The Step Family

*To Bennie
Thanks for supporting
me on my Dream I will
remmember you always
Sanette a Rucher
aka Carol*

The Step Family

Janette Rucker

Copyright © 2010 by Janette Rucker.

Library of Congress Control Number: 2010905410
ISBN: Softcover 978-1-4500-8595-3

All rights reserved. No part of this book may be reproduced or transmitted in any form or by any means, electronic or mechanical, including photocopying, recording, or by any information storage and retrieval system, without permission in writing from the copyright owner.

This is a work of fiction. Names, characters, places and incidents either are the product of the author's imagination or are used fictitiously, and any resemblance to any actual persons, living or dead, events, or locales is entirely coincidental.

This book was printed in the United States of America.

To order additional copies of this book, contact:
Xlibris Corporation
1-888-795-4274
www.Xlibris.com
Orders@Xlibris.com
63492

I would like to thank God first, then my parents Robert and Janette Andrews, next my siblings Earl, Micheal Jerry and Linda my aunts and uncles, neices nephews sister in laws and brother in law and my cousins and my best friends Benita Andrews, Vernal (Itsy) Gibson and Wanda Dixion and Vivian Taylor, love you Ladies. More thanks to my church family. Special shout outs to Tia Andrews Sara Steward and Rosie lester for helping me type my books. Special thanks for my nephew Bendrea Andrews for making the covers much love Dre and also thanks to my friends and last but not least my husband Robert Rucker. I love you baby. JAR.

Contents

FROM THE AUTHOR 9

ABOUT THE BOOK 11

PROLOGUE 13

CHAPTER ONE	ONE SHOT....................................	15
CHAPTER TWO	THE BALLER	20
CHAPTER THREE	THE TEAM	26
CHAPTER FOUR	THE TRICK OR THE TREAT?.....	32
CHAPTER FIVE	THE INTRUDER	35
CHAPTER SIX	"BEAUTY IS IN THE EYE."	41
CHAPTER SEVEN	LOVE IS BLIND............................	47
CHAPTER EIGHT	FAMILY TIES	56
CHAPTER NINE	YOU MADE YOUR BED SO LAY IN IT	63
CHAPTER TEN	HOME IS WHERE THE HEART IS	70
CHAPTER ELEVEN	DON'T BE A PICTURE BE A PERSON	76
CHAPTER TWELVE	WHOSE YOUR DADDY?................	81
CHAPTER THIRTEEN	ON THE RUN...............................	85

ABOUT THE AUTHOR.. 91

FROM THE AUTHOR

THIS BOOK I dedicate to all the so called STEP FAMILIES hoping wishing and praying that they would grow to love each other as a whole instead of something separated, because one day those worthy will all be together in Heaven as one family.

ABOUT THE BOOK

THE STEP FAMILY is about two families from different sides of the track trying to mend from Ex's and bond into one family. Joshua grew up in foster homes until a wonderful Christian family brought him into their home and showed him what a real family was about and made him vow to always be there for his children unfortunately his trophy wife whose sole purpose of life was to be beautiful and marry rich but found out money bought diamonds and furs but it didn't buy happiness. Rita on the other hand not the beauty queen but having a beautiful heart that Joshua couldn't see growing up she married a man that was overlooked by the pretty girls until he got a few of Rita's dollars in his pocket and decided instead of a beautiful heart he wanted that beautiful face and body leaving Rita and their children and a chance for Rita to find her real prince but is love enough to keep these two step families together?

PROLOGUE

WHILE AS BOTH girls sitting opposite from each other was glaring at each other angrily. Joshua and Rita looked at them and then each other wondering why these two girls looked like they wanted to get up and start fighting. "Ebony I'm glad you came down to eat with the family, everything will be great just wait and see." Joshua said. "Dad you made me come down stairs but you can't make me like these people!" Ebony yelled. "These people you act like we are a bunch of niggers and your some white master of a plantation!" Kara yelled back. "Well I'm not white, but" then Ebony stopped and gave Kara a look like she was beneath her. "Mama I'm sorry but I'm gonna hurt this girl if she says another thing about us!" Kara yelled. "Look you might be coming in the family but I can't let you go hurting my sister." Josh interjected. "I'm not scared of you JJ Jr. I'll take you on too!" Kara yelled and then the three teenagers started arguing while the parents were trying to break it up. Little Joey started crying and the sweetest thing happen Tommy sitting next to him hugged him and said. "Your still my brother" and wiped his eyes. Rita saw this and it brought her to tears. "Look at these babies their acting better than you so called grown teenagers." Joshua saw how Tommy was comforting Joey and it gave him a strange feeling how this boy that doesn't even know Joey that well can show him genuine love when Joshua was just going with the flow still not able to accept this child as his son. He was humbled.

CHAPTER ONE

ONE SHOT

JOSHUA STOOD AT the foul line; the score was now ninety-nine to ninety nine, and no more time left on the clock. Joshua had one more shot to take. This was the champion ship game. Joshua played on the Houston Rockets and his team was playing against the New York Knicks. The two teams had played six games both had three wins and this was the last one. Everyone was yelling One shot! One shot!

Joshua a six foot seven handsome light skin brother with a short fade and smooth face and dark brown eyes and sparking white teeth stood at the foul line sweating. Joshua knew this would be his last game now at thirty-eight years old he had played for twenty years and now was ready to retire. Joshua coming straight out of high school going right into professional basketball and he was glad he could get into the game at such an early age, but ashamed that he was pushed through high school some teachers overlooked the fact he was lacking in his education skills, but knew he was destine to be one of the best basketball players ever, and they didn't want to be known as one of the teachers that held him back from going into the pros, so Joshua skidded by.

The last time out was over Joshua could hear his team members yelling One shot! One shot! Knowing how bad they wanted the championship ring and all the money and glory that came with it and you would think that would be all Joshua wanted also, but Joshua unfortunately had other things on his mind more important things, wondering why he was even there when he had so much more important things going on the outside. Then the ref blew his whistle. Joshua took the ball bounced it on the floor a few times, then brought the ball up ready to take the last shot of his career, then his mind took him back to how he got to this point.

Joshua could remember back when he was five-year-old and how he was living in one foster home after another in the dark side of Chicago. Some were good some were bad, where the foster parents was only looking for a pay check, not understanding this was a child that needed a home, and a family to love him back. Those was the hard times as a young child wondering what he did wrong that made his mama and daddy not want him. Often getting jealous of the other children that had their parents who kept them. Joshua went through the taunts of the kids who would make fun of him, telling him he was an orphan or a bastard child. Through the years growing up Joshua now at ten years old, wondered if his parents even thought about what he might be going through and if they even cared. Then the day came when he moved in with the Jones.

Reverend Greg Jones, who everyone called The Rev, who was a stocky dark man of forty years of age and was the Preacher of a mid size church of about two hundred members. The Rev's wife was Mama Kelly a large brown skin woman, who was so fancy with her big hats and outfits and shoes to match that people overlooked her weight because she knew how to dress it up. The couple had one son Ben who was twelve at the time when Joshua came into their lives. Joshua was first standoffish thinking and wondering how long before he was going to be moved again. Joshua got into his mind not to fall in love with this family, because like the rest after he would get to feeling like he had a family then he would get yanked away to another home. After being crushed so many times Joshua told his self not to let his guard down, but this family was different. Rev Jones was a man, who loved his family and his church, but first he loved God and his wife was his first lady, and best friend. Mama Kelly who loved the lord also and was bringing up their son Ben who at an early age got saved baptized and was growing up blessed. Ben was a good child and he stayed in church and loved it and he also was good at school and made his parents proud. Then one day The Rev thought about the other children that may not have had parents in their life to help them get through all the problems that come with growing up. That could have been his son but, Ben was busy trying to get the gang members into church instead of trying to be one. Rev Jones seeing all these boys with no fathers choosing substitute, the gangs as family. Then watching how it only led them to gang fights, drive by's jail and death. The Rev talked it over with his family and decided to help a child that needed help so when child services placed Joshua in their home, they grew to love him. Rev Jones could see Joshua had some issues that was understandable and was going to help him grow up in be the man he was supposed to be. Mama Kelly was gonna love him out of all his issues, this boy needed a family and a home and she could see the sadness in him. Ben loved having a brother and couldn't wait to show him about the goodness of the lord, and his life was good because he loved the Lord and had spirit filled parents and he wanted to share that with Joshua. It took some time and some battles before Joshua couldn't fight all the love he was getting from this family and the church. This was different at the other homes, only a few times he got to go to church, but this family had him there three times a week, but he found his self loving it. The other saved kids made it enjoyable with the singing and dancing; it was too good to be true. So after a year of living with the Jones, Joshua asked sadly. "So when do I have to leave?" "When you get eighteen in grown, because if it's okay with you, we all Mama Kelly and Ben want to adopt you into our family." The Rev said as the tears fell from his eyes and he was unable to contain his self. Joshua was finally getting a family a mama and a daddy and a big brother. Not used to having or being loved Joshua just stood there not knowing how to accept it. The family knew though and they all gathered around him and hugged him. Mama Kelly was crying now tears of joy. Ben excited and happy that now he has a younger brother to grow up with and Rev Jones was thanking God for bringing Joshua into their lives.

The boys started off bonding Ben took Joshua to school with him to Belmont grade school and being Joshua was moved around so much he never stayed in one school long enough to get the education he needed so he was having problems with his classes, but when it came to gym it was a different story. Joshua was now twelve and Ben was fourteen years old in his last year of grade school. Ben was playing on the basket ball team and was very good and at home Rev Jones built them a net outside the house, where Ben was surprised how good Joshua was. Joshua didn't get to play much of anything coming from home to home, but when he got a chance he loved it and growing up so tall he was better than all the other kids were. Ben couldn't wait to show his coach how good his brother was.

The first day Ben brought Joshua to meet Coach Stevens, a fourtyish white man who used to play pro, but now was a teacher for the grade school he was noticing how tall Joshua was but after seeing a lot of tall children that came to his court but couldn't play he wasn't amazed. That was until he gave Joshua the ball and Joshua shot ten shots into the basket. Ben was so proud of his brother, he smiled at the coach who had his mouth wide open overwhelmed and excited. "Oh, boy we got us a gold mine, this kid can play!" The coach said to his self. The coach couldn't wait to put Joshua on the team. Their team was always last which was a hard blow for the coach to handle, being he was a pro baller, but they were kids and he didn't want to have them so into the games that they would have problems dealing with failure. Especially since most of them wouldn't ever be playing ball, but Joshua was different. Coach Stevens could see his potential and knew he could grow into a great player. First he would need the right training and hopefully stay away from the gangs that were robing all the talented kids from the game. Coach Stevens worked with Joshua after school, because they were ranked numbers ten and they were to play the number one team. There was a rival between the two coaches because the coach on the other team never played pro, but would joke with the other coaches how Coach Stevens was the only professional that played the game but had the worst team so this was a bit personal and now he had a secret weapon Joshua Jones.

The day of the game the Rev and Mama Kelly was there plus a lot of the church members was at the school to cheer on Ben and Joshua. "Are you nervous Josh?" Ben asked while they were both in the locker room waiting for the game to start. "Nah, I love to play and daddy and mama is out there and we got to make them proud." Joshua said happy to be able to finally say he had a daddy and mama. "Yeah, but there's a lot of church girls out there too, you know you want to be the man." Ben laughed. That didn't hurt that a lot of the girls from the church was there but being able to finally have parents that was proud of him was much more important to him.

The game started out with Gilmore School moving well a head of Belmont. After the first half coach Stevens still hadn't put Joshua in the game so at half time they were twenty points behind. Everyone was wondering when the coach was going to put Joshua in. The beginning of the third quarter Coach Stevens finally sent Joshua in. When Coach Turner saw Joshua come in he noticed that this was a tall kid, but didn't expect to see what happen next. Joshua and Ben were like a tag team. Ben would serve Joshua the ball and Joshua was putting up lay ups, shooting three pointers and every time he was on the foul line he would nail the shot. Coach Stevens was so proud he was almost busting out his shirt. The family and the church took over the school with all their yelling and screaming for the Jones brothers that only helped them even more to show off. Their parents were beaming with pride. After Joshua got into the game there defensive play held the other team down to only a few more points. Joshua was stealing the ball in swatting any ball the other team tried to get to the basket. Coach Stevens's strategy was to let Joshua sit out the first two quarters, so he could play the next two, and he did. When the game was over Belmont had won by ten points and their school exploded, being it had been a long time for a win and they beat the best team out there. "Where did you get that kid from?" Coach Turner asked Coach Stevens. "Wouldn't you like to know I'll be seeing you in the winner circle" Coach Stevens smiled then went in celebrated with his team. The rest of the year their team went on to win the championship, and Joshua was the talk of the school and all the girls from school and church wanted to be his girl.

THE STEP FAMILY

"Boy, you got to watch out you got skills and even being so young we got calls from scouts looking for good players like you, because they see how your going to be a great talent in the league and they want you." The Rev said. "And the females see the dollar signs and is going to be throwing everything but the kitchen sink at you, so you better use that big head and keep that little one locked up!" Mama Kelly said. "Mama!" Joshua yelled embarrassed. "Now mother let me talk to the boys about the birds and the bee's." The Rev tried to explain. "You go a head in talk about the birds and the bee's, I'm gonna tell them about the snakes and the chicken heads, all those hot pants, money hungry females out to get my boys." Mama Kelly expressed. After that the family sat down at the living room table in talked about sex. The parents explained that as Christians they hoped that the boys would wait to get married, and that they didn't have to be pressured into having sex, because others were doing it. And the potential of Aids and having babies had to be explained to make sure they knew the consequences of UN protected sex. The boys listen then got to ask questions about sex without being ashamed. "See mother that's how you do that, people ought to talk to their children about these thing, instead of them trying to go out in find out about it themselves in getting caught up in problems." "Yes, daddy, problems we would have to deal with later." Mama Kelly said

CHAPTER TWO

THE BALLER

WHEN JOSHUA ENTERED Jefferson High school as a freshman he was put on the varsity basketball team along with his brother Ben. Everyone came out to see the Jones brother's play and being they played at home a lot, the brothers knew how to play together. Ben knew when Joshua wanted the ball and when he was going to pass and what move he was going to make so they dominated the game. Ben also knew he was good, but he wasn't looking forward to going pro, he wasn't up to that standard and he didn't want it. Ben wanted to follow in his fathers footsteps and his calling was to Preach the word, but he was willing to help Joshua shine. Joshua was the top scorer from the day he stepped on the court at Jefferson high school.

Two years later Ben graduated in enrolled into Bible College so Joshua was alone and the other fellows wanted to shine also, so they wouldn't pass the ball much, but that didn't stop Joshua from standing out. Joshua was too good, only in the class room it was a different story, his new coach was excited to have Joshua and when he heard from Coach Stevens he was coming he was overwhelmed. Like coach Stevens without having a winning team also until Joshua got there, then they were unbeatable so he as the coach worked with Joshua and the other teachers and helped him get through. Joshua wasn't stupid, but he had a hard time with the classes having spent more time on the court then in the classrooms. After Ben left Joshua had few real friends at school, mostly the other team players was who he spent most of his time with, when he wasn't going to church and just like his

THE STEP FAMILY

mama said the girls threw their selves at him, mostly the pretty ones that thought they had a chance.

There was this one girl though Sandra Miller a tall sexy bright skin girl who was always after him. Sandra's brother was into the gangs so no one bothered her unless she wanted them to and she wanted Joshua. Joshua whose hormones was starting to kick in and he prayed to stop the urges but he was a teenager and now at seventeen and a dude and still a virgin was a little un heard of. Joshua had praying parents that took interest in what he was doing and gave him a lot of love so he didn't have to go looking else where. Unfortunately Sandra had his nose wide open, then there was this other girl Rita Walker a short brown skin short hair cute face girl, who wasn't a jet model, but she had character. Joshua noticed her at his church also, but they never spoke, she had her friends and she was always smiling, happy that appealed to him, but not as much as Sandra's sexy body. "Joshua I know you like me I can tell how you look at me, so why don't you pick me up tonight and lets go to this house party my friend is throwing." Sandra told him. Joshua never went to a house party always at church, but he wanted to be with her so he agreed and for the first time Joshua lied to his parents and told them he was going to his friend's house to study and would be home late. That hurt him inside how he had lied to them, but he didn't think they would approve of him at a party with a lot of teenagers late at night.

When Joshua got to Sandra's house he was driving his fathers Mercedes Benz that the Rev let him used which made it harder for Joshua being that he lied, but the little head was in the driver seat. Joshua had no control, so when he got to Sandra's house in saw all these gang bangers surrounded in front of the house, he prayed nothing would happen to his daddy's car. When Joshua got out the car in approached the stairs Sandra's brother noticed him right away. "Hey it's JJ the big baller, what you came her to pick up my baby sister, well I'm her big brother Anthony leader of the Black Aces" he said then the rest of the fellows did their gang sign, proud of their group. Joshua knew this wasn't the place he should be and wanted to pick up Sandra and leave quick. "Man why you look so nervous, ain't nobody gonna hurt you unless you was in another gang or if you think you was gonna get some from my little sister, then we would have a problem." Anthony said with all his crew giving Joshua the look. Finally Sandra came outside looking hot with a short sexy white skirt suit. "Girl you look like you gonna get JJ in trouble." Anthony said looking at his sister in her sexy outfit. "Anthony you mind your business!" Sandra yelled. "You are my business, look big baller I done took out dudes for less than hurting my sister so remember that!" "Look I'm not that kind of dude to go around hurting ladies." Joshua said growing up around gangs he was nervous but he wasn't no punk. After finally leaving Joshua and Sandra rode over to the party Sandra talked non-stop; she was feeling like a queen she was going to the party with one of the best ball players in the city. It didn't hurt that he was fine and as they were riding up in a hot black

Mercedes and she knew she looked good. When they got to the party the other kids was shocked to see Joshua; this wasn't his scene he was always in church. "Hey look at the church boy, Joshua you at the wrong place the church is across town." One of the party goers said that had everyone laughing. Joshua was embarrassed in front of the kids and especially in front of Sandra so he had to fight back. "I ain't no church boy, I grew up hard and still is anybody want to step to me so I can show them how hard I really am!" Joshua said strongly and knew he was wrong trying to impress these kids, trying to be something he wasn't but he didn't want to lose the chance to be with Sandra, who was very impressed. The night went on with the couple just hanging out. The other kids were drinking and smoking weed, laughing and dancing. Some were going into a room having sex, that's when Sandra made her move and started rubbing on Joshua's leg, he knew then it was time to let the big head back in the driver seat and he also remembered his mothers words. "Come on Sandra let me take you home." "Okay!" she smiled knowing the other girls were jealous wishing they were her. When Joshua got to her house she told him that her mother was gone to work so he could come in. Sandra was thinking he couldn't wait to get her to her bedroom, but she had a rude awaken. "No, Sandra, I can't go into your house and I have to be honest, I don't think I'm the right dude for you." Joshua said honestly. "What you breaking up with me, you trying to say you don't want this!" Sandra yelled then raised her blouse to expose her breast. Joshua turned around and told her he was sorry, but he couldn't take advantage of her like that and that he wouldn't be coming around anymore. "You can't do me like this, you think you can just drop me and embarrass me, I'll tell my brother you raped me and he's gonna kick your ass!" Sandra screamed then got out the car and slammed the door then went into the house. Joshua drove home thanking God he didn't fall into the clutches of Sandra, he was truly blinded by her pretty face and sexy body, but she surly wasn't the kind of girl he could take home and especially to his mama.

When he got home Joshua dropped the keys on the table said thank you to his parents who was sitting in the living room watching TV. Joshua was ashamed of what he did and was in a hurry to get to his room, and thinking how he was going to get out of the mess with Sandra, because he knew it wasn't over. Joshua kissed his mother goodnight and walked up stairs both parents looked at each other in shock; they could smell the cheap perfume, cigarettes and the weed smell. "Daddy did you smell that something's not right!" Mama Kelly expressed. "I know mother let's see if we raised our boy right." The Rev responded so they sat there saying their silent prayer, until Joshua walked down the stairs with his head down and sat down in front of them. "Daddy, mama, I'm sorry I didn't go to a friends house to study. I went to a house party with this girl I thought I wanted to get physical with, but I couldn't go through with it. I remembered what you both said I'm sorry, but now when everyone at school finds out I didn't have sex with Sandra, their gonna call me gay or a sissy." Joshua said. "Look boy let them think of you what they want, cause

THE STEP FAMILY | 23

I don't see any of them paying any bills at this house, cause their surly welcome to because we got a lot of them. None of them have fed you or took care of you when you got sick and most important they don't have a Heaven or a hell to put you in, so they don't matter. The real people that care about you will appreciate how you did the right thing, I'm proud of you son." Mama Kelly said. The Rev smiling with pride not having to say anything his lovely wife said it all.

The next day at the church Joshua and Ben was in there with the other kids having bible study when one of the kids came running in telling them the Black Ace's was outside in front of the church. "Their waiting for me I'll handle this." Joshua explained. "Not without me brother." Ben said. "No, they want me I don't want you or anyone else getting hurt." He said. "Like I said not without me baby brother." Ben expressed. "Me either" "I'm coming too." "I'm with you Joshua." "We will all go with you." Was heard from all the other fellows in the church. So when Joshua walked outside he had twenty kids behind him and Ben beside him. Anthony was outside with his seven gang members, started to laugh how these church kids was coming outside like they were going to do something, when all they had was their bibles. Anthony and his crew had their guns and when one of his boys seen all the fellows coming outside he pulled out his gun. The church boys stood their ground. "Put that away this is between me and JJ" Anthony told him. Joshua told Ben to hold on and he walked up to Anthony, now both of them face to face. "JJ what did you do to my sister?" Anthony asked. "Anthony I didn't do nothing and not because I was suppose to be scared of you, but because I couldn't disappoint my parents and I knew it wasn't right!" Joshua explained. "I know, Sandra was lying I always know, so when she told me that you got with her, I told her I was going to see you, but I only want to thank you, for not taking what I know she was willing to give up." Anthony said surprising. The two fellows shook hands then Ben offered a challenge on the basketball court. "Yeah, okay the Black Ace's against the holly rollers!" Anthony laughed and all the fellows started laughing and talking. Sandra went back to school ashamed and embarrassed, but it was what she needed to change her act. The fellows from the church made it a weekly advent with the holly rollers and the black ace's playing basket ball which was a perfect opportunity for Ben and the other church kids to minister to the black aces. Later some of them was coming to church and a few joined the church in got out of the gang, but unfortunately for Anthony a few months later he was gun down by a rival gang. Ben and Joshua were sad they couldn't get to him in time.

Joshua was now eighteen in his last year of high school and it was crazy how the scouts was after him wanting to wine and dine him trying to get him on their team. His parents wanted him to go to college and have something else to fall back on, some other skill just in case this didn't work out due to an injury. Joshua knew he couldn't go another four years of school and the teams was offering him millions of dollars and all he could think about is buying his daddy a new church. "So boy what you gonna do, now you know me and your mama would like you to go to college, but it's your choice your eighteen now, a grown man." The Rev told him. "Well you and mama took me in and adopted me and made me your son and I can't pay you enough for what you did, but I do want to buy you a new church." Joshua said happily. "Well I appreciate what you want to do and that's wonderful but we don't need a new church, and I'd like to tell you something about the difference between wanting and needing, because you'll be getting a lot of money. People don't understand sometimes you can ask for what you want but not what you need. Meaning you might want fifty dollars but need a hundred dollars, so ask for it you might get it, but if you only need fifty dollars and ask for a hundred you might not get anything. Son people are so mixed up. They might want a mansion but really only need a roof over their head. They might want a Benz but need just a hoopdy to get around. Some want a steak dinner, but really need just a bowl of noodles to get over the hunger pains and most men want a fine sexy woman but need to be satisfied with a good faithful Christian woman. The women always taking about how they want a Billy Dee, but need also to be satisfied with a hard working God fearing man that comes home every night with his pay check. So people can ask for what they want but should be happy to get what they need." The Rev explained. "So what you're saying is to buy what I need instead of buying what I just want." Joshua said understanding his father didn't want him buying a lot of houses and cars and diamonds like a lot of the other players do.

Joshua took that advice with him and was drafted to the Houston Rockets and given that first paycheck for ten million dollars. Joshua went wild; he grew up poor until he moved in with his new family. So this was exciting to be able to buy anything you wanted. Joshua first bought a big mansion with eight bedrooms with white marble floors, pure gold fixtures, and white furniture. That mansion had everything from swimming pool, theater and gym room and a four-car garage that was filled with a jeep range rover, a Benz and a fully custom sport car and a working truck. The parents tried to refuse but Joshua wouldn't allow them to not take a big huge check. "Now daddy, I didn't buy you what you want, I'm giving you this check to buy what you need." Joshua said. "Good baby cause I need a new dress and a new hat and I really need some new shoes!" Mama Kelly laughed. "Okay mother I'm trying to teach the boy not to buy unnecessary things." "Oh contra husband God said he would give you the desires of your heart, it's in the bible it's the word." Mama Kelly said. Joshua just smiled at his daddy knowing not to get in the middle of this and the Rev just had to shake his head, because his wife knew the word and how she used the word to get her a new dress was unique. Mama Kelly didn't want to throw the word at her husband but she wanted him to allow Joshua to be able to enjoy his money without feeling guilty, and even though she talked like she spent a lot of money on personal items for her she didn't. Mama Kelly was always suited up being a pastor's wife she had to be dressed up from top to bottom. Home though was first and she took care of it and had to ease up her spending when Ben went to college and they had to help with his schooling, but no more Joshua couldn't wait to give Ben a big check to pay for the rest of his college. Ben was so taken back with generosity that Joshua had showed him.

CHAPTER THREE

THE TEAM

THE FIRST DAY Joshua entered the stadium to practice with his new team he was a little nervous, everyone expected him to take this team to the championship. Joshua was the first draft choice and dominated his high school years and people expected great things out of him that's why he was getting all that money, so Joshua knew he had to deliver. Joshua went through practice and showed the team why he got paid so much money, they were impressed with his skills. The coach Walker was so happy when he heard their team would be getting Joshua. All the teams wanted him and Joshua teammates liked him, and were making him feel at home, but there were two fellows that attached to Joshua.

Lewis Nelson a tall seven foot country light skin brother and Donta White a bald dark skin man who was one of the guards on the team. Both of them were on the team for over two years and knew the city of Houston and were ready to take Joshua to all the hot spots. "J we are big ballers we can go anywhere we want and get star treatment." Donta said. "Yes, man and the females their all over us, we can pick whoever we want." Lewis added. "Look fellows I'm not into picking up any fast women." Joshua said but before he could explain, both Lewis and Donta stepped back and looked at each other in a strange stare. "Look J, if you gay that's your gig we ain't gonna knock you, just I wont be taking no showers by you." Donta said shocked. "I'm not gay I'm saved." Joshua said "Oh, you a church boy that's cool, more women for us." Donta laughed with Lewis and Joshua had to join in with his two new friends.

THE STEP FAMILY   27

After a year of playing Joshua was now nineteen and getting lonely he went out on a few dates but most of the women wanted to be a baller's wife. Joshua met a lot of fakes telling him what they thought he wanted to hear and offering him what they thought he wanted, until he met Tina Malone. Tina was a beautiful mixed young lady her father was black and her mother was white. Tina had long hair and a petite sexy body. Her father Bill Malone who had a high position working with the basketball league, once a player his self for the team was throwing a party for the team, at a big luxury hotel to celebrate the team making the playoffs. "Man why are we here we ain't won no championship yet?" Lewis asked sitting at the table with Joshua and Donta, who would rather be at a booty shaking house party than this stuffy up tight boring party, but it was for the team and they had to come but they didn't like it. Joshua thought it was funny watching his two friends squirm, then he saw her.

"Wow, that's a fine woman over there." Joshua said. "Oh, that's Tina Malone, Bill's daughter she is stuck-up I tried to give her a chance at me but she turned her pointy nose at me." Donta laughed. That appealed to Joshua that she wasn't star struck and through the whole advent Joshua couldn't keep his eyes off of her. "Man you looking at that girl like she's a bean pie and you're a Muslim, just go talk to her." Donta told Joshua. "No I'll wait till the time is right." Joshua said nervously. "The time is right, right now, cause it ain't right for a young dude like yourself walking around all locked up." Donta said. "Yeah J you got to let that little solider out it ain't normal." Lewis added. The fellows all started laughing at Joshua for being a virgin. "That's okay laugh, but un like you two I don't have all these women out there mad at me because I slept with them in lied and told them I loved them." Joshua said "That's their problem, they know what they're getting were ballers, we travel around the world, how do they expect the soldier isn't going to come out for duty." Lewis said. "Yes the way I look at it, the females are helping their country. "Donta laughed. "Donta you're stupid, how can you say your helping the country by sleeping around?" Joshua asked "Check it out if we get pleased, we play better, if we play good then lot of fellows get enjoyment. And what do you think all the solider boys are listening to out there on the battle fields, us, so we got to keep them happy, so the females have to keep us happy it's there duty." Donta explained. "That's about the stupid is reason I ever heard for sleeping around." Joshua shot back. "Suit your self but I see a little lady looking at me and knows that she's about ready to serve her country tonight!" Donta laughed then left. Lewis not wanting to be left out got up to go to see whom he could enlist. Joshua shook his head, his friends was young and wasn't brought up in church, so being talented in sports and making all that money had them looking at women as objects of pleasure instead of women with hearts.

Deep in thought Joshua didn't notice that now he had a visitor standing next to him. "You stared at me all night and I waited for you to come over but you didn't so here I am, and mind you I don't usually walk up to a man." Tina said smiling looking beautiful. "And you shouldn't, your breath taking, my name is." "Please, I know who you are Joshua Jones, all star player for the Houston Rockets, my daddy is Bill Malone he works for the team." Tina said. "Mr. Malone was a good player you must know a lot about the game growing up with a father that played." He said "No, I stayed home, went to school and hung around my mother mostly." Joshua thought that was odd and after having a long conversation with Tina, he found out she was so sheltered. Tina grew up with a silver spoon in her mouth, and that she was a little spoiled, but she was beautiful and had a sexy appeal that was driving Joshua nuts.

After that night Joshua and Tina was either talking on the phone or together everyday. Joshua thought he was in love and wanted what his mama and daddy had a complete family. No more dating strange women, and living through those lonely nights. Joshua wanted a wife and Tina wanted a husband, but not any husband. Donta didn't appeal to her because he wasn't making the kind of money she was used to and he couldn't give her what she was accustom to. That was big homes, cars diamond all the finer things in life, and any man that couldn't reach that standard they weren't marriage material. Joshua Jones was making millions and that's what she wanted. So first Joshua talked it over with his parents who asked if they could meet this young woman and that he had to make sure he asked her daddy first. Joshua was nervous but one day after practice; he showered in walked up to the office part of the stadium to talk to Bill. When Joshua walked inside the office all the head executives was excited to see him they were shaking his hand and telling him how good of a job he was doing for their team. Finally Bill came out his office and he was so proud that Joshua was dating his daughter. "Sir Can I talk to you alone for a minute?" Joshua asked. "Sure son, come in my office." Bill said proudly, then both men sat down and Joshua was sweating more now then he was at practice. "Calm down boy, I know what you're here for and you got my blessing to marry my little girl." "Thank you sir, and I'll be a good husband and treat her right." "I know you will, your like me son, I married a white woman and Tina is more white than black and that's what you need by your side a woman that will make you look good instead of one of those money grubbing sisters." Bill laughed. Joshua didn't think it was funny, not at all. "Sir no disrespect but I'm marring Tina because I love her, and to put down our black women is like putting down yourself. You had a black mother, and I do and without them it wouldn't be us." Joshua explained to him. Bill apologized but it was too late, Joshua had him pegged and was happy he was marring Tina and not her family. Unfortunately Tina's mother Pauline Malone was so stuck up in snobby also. The times Joshua came to their big fancy mansion that was bigger than his and had all the rich expensive items in it, it was a showpiece. Joshua felt uncomfortable there it didn't feel like a home and the way Mrs. Malone treated her help didn't sit

THE STEP FAMILY

well with him. Mrs. Malone had some Hispanic workers who she yelled at, Joshua couldn't wait to get of that house.

When Tina walked around Joshua's house he could see how she was making mental notes of what she wanted done. When she got to his bedroom Tina laid down on his bed, Joshua was still trying to hold out for marriage, but after laying next to her and all the kissing and hugging they had done it was getting hard. Tina had unbuttoned his shirt and pulled off her dress, Joshua wanted to say no, but the little head won this war. Joshua first time was ackward and he thought Tina was laughing at him for being so inexperience, but it didn't take long for his body to fall in place. Tina on the other hand knew what she was doing soon she had got on top of him and was making love to him, that was it Joshua was gone, she had him. After that night they were making love regularly and Joshua's boys couldn't wait to talk about him.

"So you getting some now, what about all that talk about I'm saved church boy?" Donta laughed. "We all make mistakes and I'm gonna marry her." Joshua expressed. "What!" Both Lewis and Donta said in unison. "You better be able to play ball for a long time, because a female like that will keep you working." Lewis said. Joshua laughed it off but thought about how Tina graduated from high school and how she was doing nothing but living at home with her rich parents, but that didn't matter he was in love. When Joshua brought Tina home to visit with his parents, everyone could tell she wasn't use to living in anything but upper class. "Joshua I didn't know you grew up so poor, how did you ever make it living like this?" Tina asked observing his family's home. "Baby you've been shelter too long, this is what you would call upper middle class, this is good living, now some of the other homes I lived in was bad, but this one was the best and not because the size because of the love these people showed me. They took me in and made me their own which I'll always be grateful." Tina being so spoiled didn't get it, she thought everything she got she was supposed to get. And it didn't take long for his parents to pick up on this spoiled little rich girl. "Mrs. Jones your home is so clean, your maid did a really good job." Tina said. Joshua had to fight hard not to laugh looking at the expression on his mama's face. "Child I'm the maid and the cook here." Mama Kelly told her. "Miss Tina, I know our son told you that I'm a Pastor do you go to church?" The Rev asked. "No, I do a little Buddha." Tina blurted out. "Well we do Jesus here!" Mama Kelly said then got up in went in to the kitchen. The Rev knowing his wife followed her "baby, I know how you feel, I don't know what Joshua is thinking about, this girl is clearly not mature enough to be married." "I know what he's thinking with and it's below the waist, because his heart and mind sure ain't in this." Mama Kelly sighed. "I know mother we just got to pray that he opens his eyes and maybe things will work out right." "Daddy we gonna have to fast and pray on this one." That Sunday when the family went to church Tina was diffidently out of her element. Tina couldn't understand how grown people would be yelling and jumping around like that. Joshua was glad to be back he missed his church and was happy to see his Brother Ben sitting in the pulpit with their father as the assistant Pastor. Mama Kelly was in the front sitting alone side Ben's new wife Gloria who was expecting their first child. Joshua was happy for his brother and wanted the same thing.

Deep in thought Joshua noticed Rita West now, up front singing with the praise team, still happy and leading the team in praise and worship. Joshua was happy to hear she had just got married to Matt West a member in the church. Matt and his family had been going to church for years and growing up in church they still weren't close, because Joshua could feel the jealousy Matt had toward him. Matt would often make comments to the other fellows that all the church girls were always surrounding around the big baller and a hard working dude didn't have a chance. That upset Joshua but, what could he do, he was what he was, but now he didn't have to worry Matt had married a nice Christian woman Rita and Joshua had Tina. Tina knew she had a good catch a rich handsome, ball player, she would never have to work or be poor, all she had to do is stay beautiful and get this man to the altar quick. So Tina and her mother had to work fast, they were going to have the wedding of the century. Bill wasn't happy about all the money it was costing him, but then he would never have to worry about working for the team, as long as his son-in-law was the star player, so he figured it to be an investment for his future. "Is there any reason why your getting married so quick son, why cant you wait and think about it some more, marriage is a big step." The Rev said over the phone. "I know daddy at first I wanted to get married right away but now I think I want to wait for a while, because I'm having doubts about me and Tina's compatibility, but she wants to do this now." "She would, wake up boy." The Rev commented so after that conversation Joshua talked to Tina about waiting for a little while before getting married that didn't go over well at all.

"What about all the plans, the people we told, the money we spent!" Tina yelled. "Don't worry baby I'll take care of all that, but let's wait for a while were young and it's a big step to take." Joshua tried to explain. Tina went home upset, shocked and crying to her mother. "How could he do this to me, to me. I could marry any man on that team and I picked him and he wants to put me off after I slept with him. First he wanted to get married so bad now he wants to wait, how could he!" she yelled. "Because that's what they do, their tricky, once they get the sex, the milk, they figure why marry the cow, but we got a few tricks up our sleeves." Her mother said. "What mother I'll do any thing!" Tina's mother looked at her and smiled and said "Tell him you're pregnant." "But mother, I'm not, were using rubbers." "Next time, do it without them, then tell him." "You think it will work?" "How do you think I got your father to marry me." She smiles. That night Tina threw away all of Joshua's rubbers and after dinner when they went to lay down, Tina put her actions in motion. Tina turned up the foreplay up a notch till Joshua couldn't handle it and when he went to look for

THE STEP FAMILY 31

his rubbers and he couldn't find them. Joshua was hesitant, and said, He had to go to the store to get some, but Tina told him she wanted him now and later she would be gone home then added. "This is me, we'll be okay." And Joshua wanted it so bad he figured just once would be okay.

A month later Tina dropped the bomb that she was pregnant Joshua had mixed emotions. Joshua was happy to becoming a father but he was unsure about the marriage, but then Tina cried and said she didn't want her child to come in this world, being a bastard child. Joshua remembered how he used to get called that in the foster homes growing up, he couldn't let that happen to his child. After Joshua told his parents the wedding was on and how Tina was pregnant, they weren't shocked but worried. "Funny how when JJ decided to hold off on the wedding that Tina finds out she's pregnant." Mama Kelly stated. "Mighty funny, but mother we got to let our son lead his own life in stay out of it and do what we do best, that's pray." The Rev added.

CHAPTER FOUR

THE TRICK OR THE TREAT?

THE WEDDING WAS a huge advent Tina made sure the tabloid was paying her big money to cover it, so it was to be shown all over the covers of the newspapers so it had to be fantastic. The wedding was held at the biggest fanciest convention center in town. The colors were white and lavender with gold chairs and candle fixtures. The men had on lavender suits and the ladies had on tight back less lavender dresses. The place had white roses all through out, along with white doves ready to be released at the end of the wedding. Tina had three of her snobby friends as bride's maid and maid of honor. Joshua had Ben as his best man and Lewis and Donta as groom's man. Joshua had on a white tux with a lavender flower on his lapel. Unfortunately Joshua wanted his father to perform the ceremony, but Tina was mad at the family for trying to stop the wedding the first time so she got another minister. The Rev was okay with this because he didn't feel comfortable about the wedding in the first place. So he sat up front with Mama Kelly, Ben's wife Gloria and Tina's mother. Mama Kelly had her game face on and had to apologized to God for wishing Tina would trip over her dress and break her leg before getting to the altar. When the ceremony started, Joshua walked up front to the altar with Ben where the minister was. Then came Lewis and Donta with the bride's maids. The next one to come was a cute little flower girl that walked up throwing white pedals. Then the little ring bearer walked up with the rings that cost hundred of thousands of dollars. Then it was the maid of honor after her it was Tina's turn; hand and hand with her father Bill decked out in his lavender tux. Tina walked the long trail up to her future husband with a dress that cost over a hundred grand. It was pure white with real diamonds around the cuffs, the dress was back less and had real white fur outside her long six foot trail it was low cut in the front with real white pearls sprinkled in the front of her veil. Last was a solid gold hairpiece with diamonds and pearls on it and Tina was glowing as she walked the long trail. There was over two hundred people there and Tina was making sure everyone saw how beautiful she looked and was getting all the pictures to show her off. Joshua was kind of reluctant, but had to admit his woman looked beautiful. Bill like his daughter loved the spot light and even though it cost him a pretty penny he was glad to see his little girl getting married and to a man that could take care of his daughter like she was accustom to.

The wedding went off without a hitch everything was perfect. The reception was elegant with all the finest foods, caviar shrimps, lobster and the most expensive Champaign. Mama Kelly tried to have a conversation with Tina's mother about their grand child that was coming but got the brush off, Tina's mother said a few words then walked away. Then went up to Tina and whispered something in her ear, then both women gave her a look that made her worry about her son. After the reception the couple flew to Paris France and had a two-week honeymoon. Tina loved France and all it's elegant, but Joshua would have been happy to be at home with family having a barbecue, and watching TV. But for his wife and the mother of his child to come he was willing to do anything to make her happy.

Shortly after they got back from their honeymoon Joshua got a shock that changed his feelings when Tina told him she wasn't pregnant and that she had thought she was because she had missed her period. "Man that's the oldest trick in the book, and you fell for it." Donta said to Joshua, when he and Lewis were all in the locker room after practice. "You don't think she would make up a lie like that?" Joshua asked. "Are you married now, enough said, Man, I would have been married over twenty times if I fell for that bull shit." Lewis said. So after that things was not happy at the newlywed's home. Joshua felt now he might of got tricked and was upset and felt stupid not making sure he saw a test, so the relationship was going down hill and it didn't help that Tina didn't believe and getting what you need she got what she wanted, everything she wanted. "Why would you need five colors of the same purse and to spend a thousand dollars on a purse, that's more than some people earn a month working." Joshua yelled at Tina looking over the bills. "Look Joshua I'm your wife and I can't go around looking shabby, can you imagine what the tabloids would say if I was seen walking around with the same old purse!" Tina yelled back. "All I know is things got to change around here or else!" "Or else what!" Tina yelled back knowing now that she was his wife it was a different story, but still she needed some advice because she didn't want to lose this nice life style, she had it better here than when she was at home with her parents.

"Mother, he's acting up again what do I do?" Tina asked. "Do what I did when your father was giving me static about my spending, I had you." She laughed. As much as Tina didn't want to lose that pretty figure of hers she had to make sure that she would never lose her rich life style, so a few months later she was really pregnant. That, just what they needed to save the marriage Joshua was happy and proud, even Tina was starting to come along, ready to be a mother. Seven Months later Joshua Jones Jr. was born and all the parents were there to welcome this new addition. Ben was there with his wife and new baby boy Dale. Lewis and Donta came by to wish their friend good luck. Tina was still spoiled but now she had someone that needed her, so she had to step up and she tried but the nanny did most of the diaper changing and feeding. Joshua was overwhelmed; he couldn't wait to come home to be with his son.

Then two years later Ebony June Jones was born now he had two children and how he hated to leave them, but the team was always traveling and Joshua was playing his best. Being voted the most valuable player, so the bucks kept rolling in and this time he didn't care how much Tina was spending, she had given him two wonderful children. Then as the years went by Joshua was visiting his parents less and less with the games and his family and Tina didn't want her kids to go to Chicago to see his family.

As time went on the kids got older Josh Jr. now twelve and Ebony now was ten years old. The couple was having problems again and the strain on the marriage had taken its toll. The couple would argue all the time. Tina was upset because she was left to take care of the children while Joshua was always away traveling working. Joshua was upset because even though she was home, she wasn't AT home, always at the spa, exercising or going to lunch with her friends or her favorite pass time shopping. The kids rarely saw their mother or their father, being raised mostly by nannies. The nanny kept changing due to Tina, who expected them to be there twenty-four seven. Most of them quit after a few months. Tina was still so immature having been spoiled all her life, so when Jack Cook came to the gym one day it changed her life.

CHAPTER FIVE

THE INTRUDER

JACK WAS SO built and fine he was a creamy brown skin man with long braids and a goatee, he was more like an eight pack. Jack would constantly flirt with Tina when she came to the gym. "Baby girl you sure look fine, then you have to, to keep that big baller husband you got." Jack said. "I don't do this for him I do this for me, I like looking good." Tina told him. "Yeah right when ever you get tired of being the trophy wife let me know." He said back to her. Tina laughed to herself Jack was fine, sexy exciting but she found out he was only a bouncer at one of the fancy clubs down town, and even if she thought about risking her marriage it wouldn't be for a poor man, but he was interesting she thought.

Time went on Tina found herself going to the gym more often just to see Jack, until one day Jack came in with a young sexy white woman, who was smiling all in his face, while he was helping her train. Jack knew what he was doing he was working out his plan to make Tina jealous and it worked. Tina was so upset when she got home she didn't talk to anyone she just went straight up stairs to her room. "Are you okay, is there something that's bothering you?" Joshua asked concerned about his wife, never seeing her look so sad. "No, I just want to be left alone." Tina said not wanting to be bothered, and she surly couldn't talk to her husband about how there was a man that had her going through emotions, she never went through. With Joshua she knew what she wanted and had it planned from the start. Jack was different, he open something up in her that had her confused.

The next few days she stayed away from the gym, then she got rose's sent to her house with a note. "Please don't stay away long you don't want to lose that sexy body you got JC." "No he didn't!" Tina said to herself mad but happy at the same time. Later at the gym "Are you crazy sending flowers to my house, what if my husband would have been home!" Tina yelled with mixed emotions. "I had to take that chance, I missed you." "It didn't seem like you miss me the other day, where's your little Barbie doll." "Oh her she means nothing, I'm a fine brother, women want to get next to me." "I know I can see why." Tina said. And both of them knew it was on, that afternoon Tina spent it in a luxury hotel room making love to Jack. Afterwards she was ashamed and there were times she couldn't even look at Joshua, but she couldn't stop. Tina was in love with Jack and Jack knew it. After months of training in the hotel room Jack finally made his move and told Tina he was going to have to move away because he was going to be evicted out of his apartment, so Tina couldn't have that so she paid it up. Then Jack needed a car to meet her, then he needed clothes and money and being she had so much Tina didn't mind, she was so in love with this man that she didn't care until two months later and found out she was pregnant.

Tina thought back and she didn't think it was Joshua's baby, because he was always gone and there was times she had sex with Jack without a rubber, not thinking lost in the moment, now she didn't know what to do. "Are you crazy, how did you let this happen you want to get thrown out in the cold streets behind a broke thug, get rid of the baby!" Her mother yelled. "I'm sorry I couldn't help it, I love Jack." "Look Tina I know how you feel and like you I've had my share of men to take care of my needs, because all you father could do was pay for them, everyone has their place. Get your pleasure, but you don't fall in love, and you surly don't get pregnant, and I'll go with you to get the abortion." Tina hung up the phone her heart was broke, she cared about Joshua but she didn't love him like she did Jack and she didn't really know whose baby this was, but looking at Josh Jr. and Ebony she knew she couldn't get rid of the child. When Tina told Jack she got a shocking response. "Look if you have to have this child make sure your husband thinks it's his, you don't want him throwing you out." "Why Jack because it would stop your money flow, and I couldn't take care of you that's why you don't want to except being a father to my child!" "Let's be real your husband a multi millionaire, I don't got it like that, why cant you have both of two worlds, he can take care of you financially and I can take care of you emotionally. Jack knew just what to say. Tina being spoiled wanted it all so this child would be Joshua's no matter what. Joshua was shocked and happy because he didn't know Tina wanted another child, being so cold he thought this would pull their marriage back together.

Then Joshua started getting more bills and found out one was from a men's store and when he checked it out he found out that it was thousands of dollars of his money spent there at this store, he never been to. Tina bought him clothes sometimes, so he dismiss his thoughts, he was having another child and the team was right in the middle of play offs. There were four teams left, so he had a lot on his plate.

Weeks went by and their team loss the championship coming in second, Joshua was taught long ago by his father to do your best and control the game and not let it control you. When the team lost all the fans and teammates were upset at the loss but Joshua was just looking forward to his new baby to come. Joshua had his agent cancel all the in coming jobs so Joshua could stay home while the team was on break. Josh Jr. and Ebony was happy to have their father home with them everyday. Joshua took the kids out every where, to the park, movies, but mostly the family just hung out at home bonding. Tina felt closed in, usually Joshua was gone so much she could easy get out and go where ever she wanted, now with him at home all the time, Tina couldn't get out and she was starting to show and had to stay home. There were good times the whole family had together and Joshua was very attentive to Tina, but she missed Jack and would sneak away and wire money to his account. Joshua told the family that he wanted to take the whole family back to Chicago to visit his parents and his brother Ben after the baby was born.

Josh Jr. was a good kid, tall like his dad, he looked just like him, but there were two difference traits they had between them. Unlike Joshua, Josh was smart, a top A student. Josh loved reading and science was his favorite class, but when it came to basketball, he wasn't very good. Which was hard for him and his father who tried to practice with him at their home court but Josh Jr. didn't have a passion for the sport and really got it bad at school. Everyone expected him to follow in his father's footstep and be a big baller. Not only did he not play that well, he didn't want to but Josh kept trying because he thought that's what his father wanted. Ebony was like her mother a spoiled little girl growing up with everything but the needed attention from her parents. So she was spoiled and mean. The help and the nannies hated that little girl, because she wanted everything yesterday and anyone saying no to her would get them fired immediately. Joshua knew she was a hand full but that was his little girl and he loved her. Tina was no help she wouldn't allow the kids to visit much with his family back home so Ebony didn't have anyone to learn from and the school she went to was a private school where all the kids were rich and spoiled.

Months went by and little Joey Jones was born a small child and Joshua was so happy to have another son. Tina looked at the baby and she knew that the baby was Jack's. Joshua was staying at home more now that Lewis had retired and Donte was traded to another team so his family was all he had. So after having the baby, Tina was at home working off her baby fat. Joshua often wondered why Tina left the house to go to the gym, when they had a gym at their house. Tina told him she liked getting out the house and working with a trainer at the gym and later Jack came into her life, that part Joshua didn't need to know. Soon as she could Tina was back seeing Jack. Jack was over joyed to have Tina back at the gym, so they continue their love affair.

Joshua was back playing and after five more years Joshua was thinking about retiring. Josh Jr. was seventeen, Ebony was fifteen and Joey was now five years old and Joshua had lost so much time with the kids, always being away. The time he spent away from Tina had got to the point that they were more like roommates then a married couple. Joshua figured once he retired, he could spend more time with his family and hopefully put a spark in his marriage. Being away so much the couple didn't get much time together and when he was home, and they made love they both thought they were just doing their duty. Tina's body, belong to Jack and Joshua didn't feel any love, but hopefully after he retired he could mend their marriage. Then one day Joshua arrived home early and decided to go to the gym to pick up his wife and take her to lunch, but she wasn't there and he found out that she rarely came by to work out anymore. Joshua thought back over five years ago when he had doubts about his wife infidelity. So he went back to the men's store and found out that his credit card paid for most of the clothes bought from the store was for Jack Cook. Joshua knew something was up but he wanted to make sure before he accused his wife of cheating.

That day when she came home late all dressed up to the hilts. "Hello baby I missed you, where have you been Tina?" he asked Tina jumped surprised to see her husband. "I've been to the gym and I missed you too." She lied then went and gave him a kiss on his cheek. Joshua was sick to think where her lips just came from. That night, he didn't reach for her and she didn't reach for him tired from her day of love making with Jack and was happy she didn't have to satisfy her husband. Joshua lay awake all night thinking about how long this affair might have been going on behind his back, and then it hit him Joey! Joshua heart started hurting thinking that Joey wasn't his child he couldn't help but noticed that Joey was darker than Josh Jr. and Ebony and some of his features were different from his brother and sister. Joshua figured Joey was taking on from the Malone side of the family, but now he knew different. Joshua was so hurt and angry with this woman lying next to him; he looked at her sleeping soundly wondering if she could ever imagine how she turned his world up side down. "How she could of done this to me?" Even after all the years he stood by her through her spoiled stuck up ways and to think how he stayed faithful to her all these years when he had all kinds of women trying to get to him. Joshua was hurt but he had to find out for sure so after the next few days he told Tina he was going out of town and would be gone the whole weekend. So after he left the house he parked down the street and waited, an hour later he saw Tina's red convertible fly by riding toward the inner city. Joshua felt his heart breaking, hoping he wasn't going to see what he thought. Tina stopped at a fancy

THE STEP FAMILY | 39

restaurant, Joshua knew he couldn't go in without being notice so he stayed in the car and waited until she came out the door and behind her was this brown skin built brother. "So that must be Jack!" Joshua thought to himself burning up inside. Joshua noticed how Tina was smiling and the look on her face was so happy, he couldn't help but feel sad that he couldn't make her feel that way. Then the anger set as he followed them as the couple walked around town shopping and all those bags Jack was caring then they went into a jewelry shop where Joshua watched from outside how Tina bought Jack an expensive watch. Joshua thought about going in there and hurting both of them. What was really worst was when the couple walked into a fancy hotel. Hours later Joshua drove home crushed and hid his car down the block and sent the kids to their rooms early. They all knew something was wrong, Joey brought tears to Joshua's eyes when he asked his brother and sister why was daddy so sad. Here this little boy who he watched come into this world that he raised, and now knowing he belonged to another man.

That night Tina walked in like usual unsuspecting happy that she just had the best day and the most wonderful night with the man she loved and glad that the kids was in bed and Joshua was gone. That's until she went to walk up stairs and she heard a voice in the dark. "Awful late for a married mother to be coming home don't you think?" Joshua said trying to contain his anger. Tina jumped in shock when she heard him and turned on the lights. "Joshua what are you doing here sitting in the dark?" Tina asked shocked. "I live here Tina remember, I work hard playing ball to pay the bills here so you can have a roof over you and our children's head. Not to feed you and your lover at fancy restaurants or buying him jewelry and clothes or paying for the room for him to screw you in!" Joshua yelled. "Stop Joshua you don't want the kids to hear!" Tina cried knowing she got caught. "Hear what how their mothers a cheat!" "Stop it, your never here I made a mistake." "Mistake is that what you call it, you spent my money on this dude, you were so busy having sex with him, that's why you kept telling me no!" "Please Joshua you wasn't reaching out to me either, who are you having sex with." "No baby don't try to switch this, I've been working hard and been faithful to you, so don't go there and now I need to know about Joey is he mine?" Joshua asked pulling no punches. Tina lowered her head in shame she couldn't speak another word. "Your silence tells me the truth finally, since I've been lied to for so long. Well baby you can tell your lover Jack to go back to the jewelry store in trade that watch in for a ring because you'll be needing a husband because I'm filing for a divorce!" Joshua yelled and went up stairs and packed his clothes and left and moved into one of their smaller homes.

The family was broken up this break up was hard on everyone. One good thing the team was on break and all the other plans Joshua had he had his agent to cancel. Tina being spoiled wanted the house and lots of money and the kids. Joshua had a long talk with his parents and they told him that it wouldn't be a good ideal for a big knock out fight, that would put him and the kids all over the papers, but Tina was greedy she wanted everything. "I'm not going to allow you to bring that dude into my house around my two kids!" Joshua said cutting Tina in the heart how he chose now not to claim Joey. Joshua was hurt but he wanted his kids he promised his self-growing up he would never leave his children the way his parents left him, but he couldn't take Joey that wasn't his child.

"What do you mean that's not your child?" Mama Kelly asked him over the phone. "Tina was cheating long time ago I suspected, but like a fool I let it go and when I asked her she said nothing." "Because maybe she doesn't know?" "Mama you seen Joey he doesn't even look like me." "Son, you don't look like me or your daddy and you may not came from me but I dare anyone try to tell me you ain't my son!" Mama Kelly said then went on to say "Son don't hurt that child by splitting him apart from his sister and brother." Joshua thought about how the kids knew nothing about this and he didn't want them to, so Joshua lawyers went in to action against Tina's high priced lawyers that her mother used when she divorced her father years ago. When Joshua's lawyers brought in evidence of Tina's cheating and how it would come out in all the papers Tina finally decided to give up the fight, even against her mothers advice. "You can't let him have the house and without the kids you won't have all that money. You know how you like all those nice thing and you won't be able to live like you used to with that cheap spousal support he wants to give you. Don't let him get away with pushing you out!" Tina mother said. "Mother Joshua lawyer said if we have a messy divorce my affair with Jack would come out and everyone would know and the kids would find out and hurt the most, I cant do that to them. And now I can quit living a lie, and sneaking around I love Jack and now I can start my own life." Tina said relieved that now she can begin again on her own. After she left her parents, then she went in got married to Joshua she never had a chance to fly and be free, unfortunately the kids would hurt the most but Tina knew they would be better off with Joshua.

So Tina moved out into one of the other houses, which was just as big and fancy. The divorce gave her millions of dollars, Joshua was very generous because she was the mother of his children and he wanted out. The hardest part was the effect on the children it was a lot of tears when the kids was told the divorce was final, and that their mama and daddy was never getting back together. The family was trying to mend without Tina there at the house. Tina wasn't at the other house a week before she moved Jack in with her, so he took all of her time and she wouldn't even come visit with the kids that hurt Ebony the most. Joshua did all he could, then he thought it was time to bring the kid's home to visit with his parents.

CHAPTER SIX

"BEAUTY IS IN THE EYE."

THE REV AND MAMA Kelly and Ben's wife Gloria and his son Dale who was now eighteen was all happy to have Joshua back to visit. Months had past and Joshua also felt relieved that finally he could stop living a lie, from the beginning of his marriage it was problems. The only good thing that happen in the marriage was his children and as hard as he tried, every time he looked at Joey he was reminded how Tina cheated on him and that this child wasn't his. Joshua knew he had to come to terms with this, so Joshua was glad to be back in church.

The children were shocked watching all these church folks shouting and praising the Lord. This was what he and the kids needed. Joshua was getting into the spirit even though he noticed how a lot of the women had moved closer to his seat and were grinning and smiling. They didn't know that was the last thing he wanted was another money hungry, glory seeking woman. Joshua was so past that as far back as he could remember he had women always throwing their selves at him, but there was always this one girl, Rita.

Rita never even bothered to talk to him; Joshua remembered how she use to belong to the church. So Joshua looked all around then he saw her in back of the church sitting with two children a teenage girl and a young boy. Often Joshua would turn around and watch her and her realness appealed to him. Rita wasn't a fashion model but she had a beauty about her self, he wondered if her husband Matt who wasn't there could see it. After church the family all went back to the house for dinner. Mama Kelly had cooked up a big spread of food. Josh Jr. was enjoying hanging around outside shooting hoops with his cousin Dale with Joey out there hanging with the big boys. Ebony sat by herself by a window in the living room, hoping to go home soon, even though she didn't have many friends being so stuck up and spoiled. Joshua hoped Ebony would change being around real people. "What's wrong with that girl?" Mama Kelly asked. "She's like her mother spoiled and stuck up, and she's mad about the divorce." Joshua explained. "Well we need to deprogram her before it's too late and she grows up like Tina."

The next day Mama Kelly had Joshua drive her to the beauty salon, when they walked in there she was Rita along with another woman and a fellow who had a weird hair cut and lot's of earrings all over and he was wearing make-up. "Hey big baller what brings you into my shop, Rita's hair and care you need a cut?" Rita asked with a big bright smile on her face. "Hum, if she don't do it, I'll cut it for free, my name is Glen but my friends call me Glenda, you have my permission to call me Glenda." The fellow smiled. Joshua now feeling uncomfortable said "no thanks, I got a regular barber back home in Houston I'm just here to drop off mama." Then he glanced at Rita who still looked the same just a little older, she had brown skin with only a touch of make-up, hiding her medium size frame under her big smock and her hair cut into a short fancy short style with a big inviting smile. Mama Kelly sat down at Rita's chair and told her son to come back to pick her up in two hours.

When Joshua got back to pick up his mother, he complemented Rita on her work. "I didn't know you had all those skills Rita." Joshua said. "That's because you didn't notice anything other than that basketball and all those centerfold girls, all us plain girls, you didn't pay us no attention." She laughed. He tried to laugh along with her but deep down it hurt him that he was that shallow. When they were riding home Joshua asked his mother about Rita.

Rita was smiling as she was working on her next client thinking about Joshua Jones as far as she could remember, when she was a small girl living in a home with only her mother around the poor streets of Chicago. They were poor her mother a small brown skin pretty woman often had to work two jobs to feed Rita and her two small brothers. Many men wanted to get with Rita's mother Mable who was only sixteen years older than her. Mable won many beauty contests growing up, her mother had her entering in every contest out there and usually Mable would win being so beautiful her mother would always tell her to use her looks it could get her every thing she needed in life. Mable didn't want to decide her relationships on how she looked she wanted a man to love her totally and not look at her as some kind of a showpiece. So at an early age Mable rebelled in to her mother's dismay Mable got pregnant at sixteen. Rita's father was some young thug that would hang around town with the other young boys stealing and fighting. Mable mother was so upset that Mable had ruin her chances of being a beauty queen and marring a rich man that she put her out. Mable moved in with some other young mothers until she got on welfare, five years later she had a son Norman then Monty, followed the next year. Mable didn't want her kids to see her begging for money so she worked two jobs cleaning to support her family, until she died from cancer a few years later. Rita wasn't ugly but she wasn't a beauty queen so she had to work, but it was okay, her mother had made her proud and happy. So when Rita entered Jefferson high school as a sophomore and saw Joshua Jones who was a junior, her life changed. Rita had a huge crush on Joshua, she would go in watch all his games and she had his pictures and articles of him all up on her wall at her home. Then she started going to church nearby her home and saw Joshua there finding out it was his families church, that gave her more opportunity to see Joshua, but her fantasy was shot down when she found out he was going out with Sandra. Rita thought she saw something different in Joshua and that he wasn't like all the other jocks. And being he was a PK Preachers kid, she hoped he could look past the cute, sexy air brain women, that was until she overheard Sandra boasting about how she was going out with Joshua and she was going to be a ballers wife. That was it Rita went home and took all Joshua pictures off the wall and decided to grow up in come down to the real world.

Later Joshua graduated then was drafted to the Houston rockets. Life goes on Rita later graduated then went on to beauty school and while she was going to school she worked at a salon. Rita was very good she did wonders on ladies hair. The styles she did were unique and she made sure everyone had something that fit them. Rita wasn't just making money she wanted her clients happy and for them to look good. People from all around would come to see her and she one day wanted to own her own shop, so she saved her money, and had to quit school because she had so many clients. Most of the people was from the church among them was Mama Kelly Joshua's mother.

Life was good Rita had been working at the shop and still going to church where she and another member Matt West was going. Rita knew Matt and they was friend until that friend ship turned to love. Matt was an average looking young man; he was a garbage man who attended the church. What Rita liked about Matt most was that he was a church man and that he wasn't trying to go after all those pretty girls, unknowing to Rita the pretty girls didn't want to be hooked up with a garbage man. So Rita and Matt started dating, they had so much in common two average people working hard and going to church a match made in heaven. The couple had a nice small wedding at the church and life was good. And later they had their first child Kara. Everything was going well; Rita wasn't bothered how Matt was starting to change when she got her own shop and started making lots of money. Rita's Hair and Care was one of the more popular shops in town. Rita brought in her home girl from high school, Anna Burns who was a light skin skinny woman with a long weave, who was average like Rita, and hated how they were treated in high school.

Years later Matt quit his job in started working at the shop doing maintenance work and with all the money coming in Matt bought new clothes and started putting more care into his appearance. Now that he didn't have to deal with trash anymore and he liked being at the shop with all those pretty women coming in and out. It's something how money can change people. Matt started staying out late and coming home smelling like cheap perfume when Rita asked him, he would often tell her she was lucky he married her and there were times Rita believed to be lucky. Rita had a husband when so many women didn't. Times got worst and after ten years Rita had another child a son Tommy West. Rita was so happy that she overlooked the signs of Matt disrespect, until the day she was doing a clients hair who had heard a rumor that Matt was having an affair with Mildred Warner, a pretty woman who was one of the members at their church. Rita first didn't believe it until one Sunday at church she noticed how they looked at each other and turn away. Rita didn't want to admit, but now it was so bad for women, even the pretty ones to get a man so they had to settled on what they could get, so Matt had some money made him a good catch. Rita couldn't believe that people at church could do such a thing but The Rev preached that there are snakes every where like the Garden of Eden, their at the church too.

Before Rita could approach Matt about his affair he had came up to her and told her he didn't want to be married anymore and he was leaving, just like that. Rita had a ten year old daughter and a new born, she was crushed, but the pain didn't hurt as bad until the next Sunday when Matt and Mildred walked in the church like it was nothing. They sat down like they had been a couple for years, while the whole church felt sorry for Rita as she sat alone with her daughter and baby, but what brought tears to her eyes was when Kara asked. "Why is daddy not sitting with us mama?" Rita held her ground went through church then left so embarrassed and hurt. Matt was happy finally he got his beauty queen and Mildred just wanted a man and she didn't care whose man. They both walked out not caring about the mean stares they were getting. "Girl I don't know how you could go to that church and watch your husband sit with that snake. See that's why I don't go to church, I can get that kind of treatment outside I don't need to be faced with that while I'm trying to get my praise on!" Anna said and Rita considered changing churches, but she was saved before she met Matt and no matter where she went she was going to continue to love the Lord, but her heart was hurting so she prayed for an answer.

Later at her home there was a knock on her door. It was the Rev and Mama Kelly, Rita invited them in and they all sat down over coffee. "Rita we know the situation with you and Matt and it was so cold blooded how he walked in with

THE STEP FAMILY

Mildred and me and my wife could understand if you didn't want to attend our church anymore." The Rev said sadly. "Pastor I was just praying about the situation when you and your wife came to my door and I know now I got my answer. You have a caring church that cares about its members and you coming to my house today just assured me of that. I won't let them push me out." Rita told them. "That's my girl don't let them make you run, if I left every time some female made a pass at my husband, you would never see me, some people just don't care anymore." Mama Kelly expressed. "But there's some that do, you two have lifted my spirit, thank you." Rita said. As they were riding home the Pastor and his wife talked about the conversation at Rita's. "You know honey I wished Joshua could of married a nice sweet lady like Rita, Matt doesn't know what he had." Mama Kelly said. "Yes baby and I can't push people out the church, but I can preach what's on my heart. So the next Sunday Pastor Jones preached on adultery and how even in church both women and men have to pray to save their marriage, because the sanctity of marriage ain't safe even in the walls of the church. Rita sat there with her children with power that she could get through this, she could hear the other women saying to her "keep your head up and we got you." Mildred and Matt sat there looking sick, the Pastor had wiped that grin right off her face. Mama Kelly turned around and gave Rita a wink and a nod. After church Mildred and Matt were the first ones out the door.

The next Sunday they didn't show up but Matt wasn't done it was a messy divorce. Matt was greedy and wanted lots of money to keep his life style in tack and to be able to keep Mildred, who did not want anything to do with Matt's children. So on visiting days Matt was usually a no show. Rita was livid and offered him a payoff to get him out of their lives but he wouldn't take it. Rita had to sell the house and move into a smaller one to keep him from taking her shop. Then even though she had the kids she had to still pay spousal support to Matt. Rita felt life was unfair she had to sell her house and still she had to support this man who wouldn't come in see his kids. Mildred started to get nervous that Matt could walk out on her like he did Rita and she wouldn't get anything so she convinced him to marry her. Only thing once the unknowing couple got married that ended his support. Matt went back to court after his checks stopped to compel to the court about how he didn't have a income Rita smiled with triumph when the lady judge told him to tell his new wife to support him.

For the next five years Rita continued to work go to church and take care of her kids. Rita found it was hard for a black woman who wasn't very pretty or young and a Christian to get a man, but that was okay because she had her kids to keep her busy, until she saw Joshua walk back in church. Rita found out through the newspapers and the church folks that Joshua had been divorced. Tina, who didn't come to any games, she thought they were too long and too sweaty for her to sit through. So other than the papers and that one time when, Tina came to church with Joshua that's the only time Rita saw Tina and all she could say was that he finally got that beauty queen when she saw them together and went on with her life, now he was back. Then Rita woke up from her day dreaming wondering how long it was going to take before he finds another trophy wife.

CHAPTER SEVEN

LOVE IS BLIND

JOSHUA AND THE kids got back home to Houston and Ebony was thrilled. "Daddy I don't want to go there anymore, those people are boring." Ebony said. "Those people are my people and your people, that's your family baby." Joshua explained. "Their not my family and I want to call my mother." "Go a head call your mother." Joshua said but he knew what was going to happen. Tina was so busy with her boy toy and taking care of him, she was so in love with that man that she didn't have much time for her kids and Jack had no need to bond with the children even Joey who looked just like him. That hurt Tina but Jack didn't want to be faced with child support again. Tina was shocked to find out Jack had three other kids out there that he wasn't supporting. That's why Jack didn't keep a job because the court kept coming after him to take care of his kids. Now he had Tina to take care of him, and he was living in a huge mansion with a beautiful lady and all he had to do was to keep Tina happy, all the kids hated this playboy. "Mom how could you of left dad for this broke pretty boy?" Josh Jr. asked "Yeah mother daddy is so sad and lonely." Ebony said trying to make her mother feel sad for her father. "Look both of you, me and your father's marriage is over, were not mad at each other and I'm in love with Jack" Tina said. "If your so in love with him why aren't you married to him?" Josh Jr. asked. Tina wasn't that stupid she knew as long as she was single she would get spousal support and now she was getting a lot of money to live on, but it wasn't like before and like her, Jack had got use to living nice. Now she had to question Jack often about his use of her credit card, now she knew how Joshua felt. The kids unfortunately suffered the most.

Josh Jr. was on the varsity basketball team, but clearly wasn't that good but he was Joshua Jones son, and he hated the game but he wanted his father happy and did what was expected. Ebony at fifteen was a pretty freshman but not that smart. Ebony was so pampered having everything she ever wanted and the boys was all after her, she was pretty rich and she was a baller's daughter, so it made sense her first boy friend was the best player on the varsity basketball team Roy Steel. Josh Jr. was friends with Roy a tall dark built, bald young brother, who looked like he was going to go pro. Joshua was happy that Roy was a nice kid and showed him a few pointers about the game. Joshua was amazed at Roy's skills and wished that Josh his son showed that much passion like Roy, maybe he would be a better player. Josh was a little jealous of the closeness Roy and his father had. Ebony was hoping that Roy could turn out like her father and like her mother all she had to do was be beautiful, but she still wasn't happy.

The divorce was hard on Ebony and little Joey was caught in the middle a sweet boy that loved his sister and brother and daddy and mama so much. The only thing Joey was a little slow, Joshua thought he had signs of mental retardation but the doctors said he just reads different, so he had to get special help. Tina was embarrassed by Joey sometimes and was glad that Joshua took him; she had a hard time watching her son struggle with his words. Jack figured Joey was Joshua's problem. And at times it was a huge problem. As hard as he tried Joshua was still upset at the fact Tina had this child with her lover and not only were they not facing up to it they left Joey for him to take care of. Joshua felt like they were laughing in his face. Joshua thank God, he was taught better than that and wouldn't tear the kids apart. Josh Jr. and Ebony would of been crushed, but he knew one day he would have to tell them the truth about Joey, but it was too soon after the divorce, one thing at a time he thought.

As time went on Joshua was still playing ball, but it was younger players coming in and even at thirty-seven he wasn't old, but the time was coming for him to look and find something else to do. Running up and down the court for two and half-hours was wearing him down. A few months later his team was to play in Chicago, he couldn't wait to get home and visit with his family. The kids were still in school so Joshua had their nanny Miss Dorothy an older dark black woman watch over the kids while he was gone. A couple days before the game Joshua arrived home to visit with his family. They were so happy to have him home and The Rev and Mama Kelly had a few people over for a barbecue. Mama Kelly being close to Rita invited her to the advent it was a warm day, the sun was out and when Joshua got there everyone was swarming around him especially the women everyone except Rita. Rita was a down to earth woman and even though she was happy to see Joshua and what single woman wouldn't be interested in a single handsome, nice rich man, but with all those pretty women around him,

THE STEP FAMILY

49

she knew he wouldn't even notice her. The party was fun all the people enjoying themselves dancing and eating, laughing.

Rita had brought her two kids who were her joy. Kara was an average brown skin full figure girl who was sixteen and who was confident and happy. Everyone loved her sense of humor and her sassy ness. Kara was a good student and planned to go to college and study law. Tommy was six years old and like Kara he was a happy little boy. Rita made sure her children had a lot of love and attention but both children had to deal with the fact they didn't have a father. Kara was old enough to know what happen with her parent's marriage and encouraged her mother to move on. Rita smiled at how her and Kara was so tight, they could talk about anything and because of that and attending church, Kara didn't have to go looking for love from a boy or a gang, that was all through her neighborhood.

Rita was having a good time at the barbeque when she looked around and didn't see Tommy she searched all around the house until she went around the side of the house and saw Tommy shooting hoops with Joshua. Rita's heart started getting warm as she saw Joshua playing with her son something Matt never did. Tommy loved basketball and was so excited playing ball with Joshua Jones; even young as he was he knew who Joshua was. "Look mama I'm playing with JJ" what all the TV people started calling Joshua. "JJ look, I got your shoes on!" Tommy said smiling and pointing at his hundred dollar pair of tennis shoes that he told his mama he had to have. "I see son, hopefully he can teach you to play like him so you can take care of your mama!" Rita laughed. Joshua laughed at how funny Rita could be. "You know you got a good kid here." Joshua said admiring how happy this little boy was. "Yeah, I got a teenage daughter Kara that makes me proud also, where is your kids?" "Their in school and couldn't come, are you coming to the game Rita?" "No." "No!" Joshua said surprised. "No I always watch the game on TV." "We can't have that I want you to see our team whip your teams butt." Joshua joked. "I don't know we got a good team this year, our center William Fraizer is playing good and we got two new guards." Rita told him. "What, you know your game." Joshua said impressed that Rita really liked the game and wasn't faking like most of the other ladies that talk to him. They talked a long time outside about school and the game until Rita had to go and Joshua had to go to practice. Joshua met Kara and she was so down to earth, not stuffy like his daughter Ebony. "Rita you and your kids have to come to the game, I insist and I'm leaving three tickets along with the one's for my family at the gate." Tommy heard about going to the game and was so happy he was jumping up in down. Kara was happy also but she was happy how her mama was smiling ear to ear. That night before the game they had to be ready. "Mama, Glenda is coming over to do your hair and I went out and got you a new outfit." Kara said. "Why you don't think Joshua is inviting us to the game because he's interested in me, no girl I'm not his kind of woman, he likes those skinny painted up fancy women, he's just being nice." Rita told her daughter. "Well just in case it don't hurt to be ready for anything." Rita decided to humor her, but she and Joshua went way back to high school and she knew better. Then Glenda walked in; he was all decked up in his tight flashy clothes in his two-tone bright colors. "Girl I'm gonna make you look ghetto fabulist!" Rita talked him out of the ghetto look and went for the standard flat iron look, and then Kara brought her a Jean pants suit. Then her and her kids left for the stadium.

When they got there they were seated with Joshua's family toward the front. When Joshua came out on the court he saw his family and Rita and her kids, and it made him feel special. Joshua knew he had to show out and he did thirty points worth and those people yelled in cheered him on right in the middle of all those Chicago bull fans and Rita was yelling the loudest. Houston beat Chicago by twenty points. The next day at the shop Rita was working on a client when she got a call from Joshua. "I hope its okay to call I think you owe me a dinner." Joshua said. "What, how do I owe you a dinner Joshua?" and when Rita said his name all the workers in the shop stop working to hear what Joshua had to say. "Remember we bet on the game and you lost, but because I'm such a gentle man I'm gonna take you out." He laughed. "No because I'm such a lady I'm gonna cook you dinner at my home." After she hung up the phone Glenda and Anna argued about how Rita was suppose to act, and what to cook. Glenda told her to cook something light and have wine and candle lights. Anna told her to cook him a huge spread of food; "Something the little miss is never did for him then have some hard alcohol and send the kids to my house." "Thanks but no thanks I'm gonna be myself and besides he's just being friendly, you know I'm not the kind of lady he runs with." "Don't count your self out, he could be at any woman's house including mine, but he chose you." Glenda said.

When Joshua got to Rita's home he felt the warmth when he walked in the door. The kids were happy to see him and thanked him for the tickets to the game. Joshua felt so at home eating dinner with this family. The food was good Rita could really throw down in the kitchen. Afterwards they all sat down watching TV and laughing. Joshua enjoyed Rita and her kids and how well adjusted they were. Later the kids went upstairs to bed; Rita smiled how Kara gave her mother a wink. "Okay stop beating around the brush of all the places you could be, why here Joshua?" Rita asked "because I enjoy the realness of your company and what I'm looking for is a friend to talk to, I hope I didn't lead you on." Joshua was still stinging from how Tina did him. "Good now that's out the way, I can ask you what happen to your marriage?" Joshua feeling at ease and finally being able to talk told Rita the whole sad story. "Well that's another thing we have in common other than the love of basketball, Matt left me for a pretty woman that attended our church, I wasn't good enough for him." "No offense but Matt was a fool, you're a beautiful woman with

THE STEP FAMILY

51

great kids and if he can't see that he's blind." Joshua told her. Rita was getting misty. "That was the sweetest thing anyone has ever said to me thank you and I'm sorry." "What are you sorry for?" he asked. "I'm sorry of how in high school I thought of you as a some what super fiscal jock when you started dating Sandra, that girl was a gorgeous body with a rock for brains." Joshua agreed in they both laughed. They talked well into the night, then Joshua kissed Rita on the cheek and left. The next day when Rita got to the shop both Anna and Glenda was they're waiting. "Look a here, both of you here before me, this is the first I got to go outside and see if I'm at the right place." Rita laughed. "Quit playing and tell us all the dirty details." Anna asked. "Nothing dirty to tell, it was nice and he just wanted a friend to talk to, I told both of you that's all he wanted, now lets make some money." "Girl I could of stayed home and slept another hour if I knew you had such a boring night." Glenda expressed. Rita smiled thinking it was nothing boring about her time with Joshua.

When Joshua got back home, the kids was happy to see him and he decided to take Rita's advice and to spend more time with them. So he made a call to his agent and had him to cancel some projects so he could spend more time at home with the kids, but it was hard. Josh Jr. was holding back something that was bothering him, Ebony had her issues with her mother and Joey was looking more like his real father everyday and it was bothering Joshua. Being so rich Joshua had a hard time having true friends that weren't looking for hand outs and the women all they wanted was to sleep with him, so they could catch him. That's why Joshua loved talking to Rita she knew him from way back and his family and she wasn't asking for anything but friendship. They both had a lot in common and like him they both got burnt in bad marriages and had children so they had a lot to talk about. So Joshua would call Rita at least once a week. "Hello, Rita how's your week been going?" Joshua asked lying on his bed after a long day. "Hectic, Glenda got in a argument with a client about one of his ghetto fabulist hair styles he gave her, I had to fix the ladies hair all over, then Kara got some boy looking at her." "My daughter Ebony got a boy friend, but I like him, but I am nervous I don't want to be a grand daddy." He said. "I don't worry about Kara, we talk about everything, you need to talk to Ebony and make sure she knows she don't have to prove anything, you know how high school boys are." "Yes I do, if I wasn't taught better I might have got down with Sandra." "You mean you didn't?" Rita asked surprised. "No girl I was a virgin when I met Tina." Rita couldn't believe how nice Joshua was; she enjoyed his phone calls.

Weeks later Rita got a call from Joshua that the team had a cruise plan to go to the Bahamas and he needed a friend to accompany him and he couldn't think of anyone but her. "Joshua I can't go on no cruise with you, what would people think?" Rita asked. "I don't care I've been doing a lot of things that people expect me to do. I think you need a nice vacation and if I brought another woman, they would think

I'm trying to court them, you know I'm not ready for that and I don't want to go alone." After more conversation Rita decided to go with him. "Bahamas! Girl it's on like donkey con now!" Glenda yelled. "Stop Glenda where going as friends." Rita explained. "Rita if you get on that ship and don't come back with that man on your arm I'm through with you." Anna said disgusted. Kara was excited for her mother and told her to have a good time and she would watch over Tommy while she was gone." Rita knew Kara could hold down the house. Rita got ready and Joshua picked her up and many hours later they were on a ship sailing to the Bahamas. When they got to their room and open the door it had one king size bed. Rita's eyes grew wide "I'm sorry Rita I guess every room is the same and most of the people are couples, I'll order a cot for me to sleep on." Joshua said "Joshua it's a big bed you stay on your side and I'll stay on mine okay." Rita suggested "No problem if it's okay with you, now lets get unpacked and go to the deck." Joshua said. Rita met all the team members and their wives and girl friends and everyone was having a good time. After dinner Joshua and Rita walked along the ship, the night was beautiful, the stars was shinning. Rita and Joshua started feeling uncomfortable watching all the couples out there hugging and kissing so they decided to go to their room. Rita made sure against Glenda advice and wore a safe full nightgown instead of the G-string see through piece of material he wanted her to wear. As she laid down on her side Joshua was already in bed feeling uncomfortable wondering if this was a good ideal and if he should call for that cot or see if he could get another room. Until Rita started talking and made him feel at ease, they laid there and talked all night. When Joshua woke up and saw Rita sleeping soundly he felt a little different he looked at her peaceful face and she was so beautiful to him. Never had he felt so good around a woman. After Tina and a few other women he dated none of them could see past his money and status. Joshua got up and got ready when Rita woke up Joshua was sitting on the side of the bed. "Wake up sleepy head, usually when people take these kind of trips and spend this much time in bed they ain't sleeping." He laughed. "Well let me get up!" Rita said because she knew it wasn't going to be any sex going on.

That day was wonderful they ate exotic food and sat by the pool and that night they both got dressed up in went to the lounge area where there was a band, they danced and mingled with everyone. "Joshua I'm having the best time, I can't thank you enough" Rita told him excited. Joshua was happy to see Rita enjoying herself, because she was such a sweet lady, and he started to feel strange a feeling he never felt before, and it was a pleasant feeling like everything was so right. As the couple left the lounge they walked along the ship and stopped to watch the water an as Rita was talking Joshua could see the stars shinning on her lovely face he couldn't help his self, he leaned down in kissed her deep. Rita loss in the moment kissed him back, it was the best kiss either one ever had. "That was not a friendship kiss Joshua." Rita said pulling herself together. "I know, I'm

THE STEP FAMILY | 53

sorry we better get off this boat, we are forgetting about our friendship." Joshua added. That night they laid down and tried hard to go to sleep finally after hours of struggling to go to sleep they finally did, but woke up in each others arms. "Oh boy how do I explain this?" Joshua said to his self as he looked down at Rita in his arms. "I'm sorry, I must of rolled over here next to you, don't worry I'll get it together, nothing serious, don't panic Rita." Joshua said nervously. "Well I think you need to tell your little solider that, because right now he's poking me in my leg." Rita laughed. Joshua was embarrassed but had to reply. "First, he's not little and second he has a mind of his own in the morning time, I'll get him in check unless." "No, no." Rita was stopping him before he could even finish. "I'm sorry Rita I don't know what I was thinking, I'll never come to you like that again, I promise you I value our friendship." Joshua said. "It's okay, I would probably be bothered if you didn't at least think of it, I mean were here on this romantic ship, but then you have your choice of any woman why would you choose me." Rita said. "Rita stop putting your self down, you're a beautiful woman inside in out, now you get up first, and let's go enjoy our trip, but I have to wait for my soldier to calm down." Joshua laughed. Rita laughed till she cried both of them laying there enjoying each other. The rest of the trip it was no more problems until it was time to leave. Joshua gave Rita a big hug before she got on the plane to fly back to Chicago. Rita shed a few tears thinking how wonderful this man made her feel and when she thought about how one day he was going to find a woman and their friend ship would end had her heart hurting.

Joshua got back home and the kids were so happy to see him, he took them all out and bought them nice things. Then that night he laid in bed and dreamed of Rita. When Rita walked in the shop the next morning, Glenda and Anna was there waiting for her? Anna took Rita's right hand. "Hum, no ring." Then she started looking in her eyes. "What you doing Anna?" Rita asked "I'm trying to check if you REALLY had a good time." Anna said. "Spill it, I woke up early so I could get here before the clients to hear all the four one one, so let's have it." Glenda said all excited. "We had a nice time." Rita responded "No huh, huh sister girl what about the room?" "We had one room" Rita said "One bed or two?" Glenda asked "One" Rita said and smiled. "Yes, yes, now I know it was on." Glenda smiled "No, it wasn't on we just slept, that's all." Rita told them. Both Anna and Glenda looked at each other and shook their heads. "I'm through with you." Anna said disgusted. "Rita you mean to tell us you had this big bed on a romantic ship cruising the night laying next to that handsome chunk of man and you did nothing." "Yes that's what happen we just slept." "See you women don't know how to get and treat a man." Glenda said "I can't be having sex, I go to church and how could I face Kara an expect her to behave." Rita explained. "Look you do what mama says not what mama do! That's what I was taught." Anna said. "Well my mama told me you can tell a child once not to do something, but if you do it your telling them a hundred times to do it." Rita told them. Glenda told Rita next time, he was going with her to show her how to get a man. Rita wondered if it would be another time.

Joshua went back to the stadium and after a long practice he stood in the shower and lots of things went through his head, then suddenly he knew what he had to do. Joshua told his agent this would be his last season and because he invested his money Joshua would not be hurting for money. Then he arranged for Dorothy to stay over, then he went to a jewelry store, caught a plane and on the way he called his parents. When Joshua got to Rita's shop and walked in Rita was overwhelmed, she was working on a client and thinking about Joshua at that moment. Joshua stood at the door smiling at her. "Hello Joshua I was just thinking about you." "I haven't stop thinking about you since our trip." He said then he walked over to her and gave her a deep kiss. The whole shop stood still watching the two. Glenda and Anna was high fiven each other. "Wow Joshua that wasn't a friendship kind of kiss." Rita said trying to pull herself back together. "I know it wasn't a friendship kind it was something a lot more." Joshua said, and then he knelt down on one knee. The client in the chair was smiling thinking "ooh wee, I wish it was me." Glenda and Anna started yelling and jumping up and down. "Rita, baby I love you and want you to be my wife." Joshua said bending on one knee holding out this huge diamond ring. Rita stood there in shock; she couldn't believe what was happening not knowing what to say. "Look JJ, if she wont marry you I surly will!" Glenda said winking at him. The whole shop was laughing Joshua looked at Glenda with that "Oh hell no!" look. Then Rita started crying and said "Yes I will marry you." Joshua took her in his arms in then they went in the back. "You see ladies I taught her every thing she knows about getting a man!" Glenda said wiping his eyes by then the whole shop was full of women crying, and then a man came in the shop and asked his wife why everyone was crying. "Somebody get a bad perm?" he asked. "No silly somebody getting married." She smiled wiping her eyes. "Yes I can see how that can make you cry I been crying for years being married to you." He joked. His wife didn't like the humor and gave him a poke to his side.

That afternoon Rita and Joshua left to go pick up the kids and tell them about the wedding to come. When Joshua walked through the halls of Tommy's school everyone was yelling his name then Tommy came out of his class and when he saw Joshua he was so excited he ran into Joshua's arms. Joshua picked him up and carried him outside where Rita was waiting. Then they drove up to Kara's high school. Kara was outside talking to her friends when Joshua walked over to her and told her that he and her mama came to pick her up. Kara was overwhelmed when all her class mates started coming outside yelling "There's JJ!" "Mr. Jones you made my week the kids will be talking about this for a while." Kara said excited. Joshua smiled then drove the family home where they all sat down and he asked the kids if they didn't mind if he married their mother. Tommy was jumping up in down, Kara started

THE STEP FAMILY

crying for her mama and then ran into her arms, now both of them crying, but the tears really started to pour when Tommy asked "Sir, can I please call you daddy?" "You sure can and Kara I wouldn't mind if you called me that also, it sounds good." Joshua said. "Okay daddy" Kara said through her tears then Joshua grabbed the whole family and hugged them thinking "now I got to tell my kids."

CHAPTER EIGHT

FAMILY TIES

"**N**O, I DON'T want another mother and what about mama!" Ebony yelled. "Baby that's been over a long time and she has Jack why can't I have someone?" Joshua asked knowing it wasn't going to go over good with his daughter. "So you two ain't gonna at least try to work it out?" Ebony asked "No Ebony we both moved on, can't you be happy for your dad?" he asked "I can, this is your life you do what you think is right and be happy." Josh Jr. said hoping that his father would understand the same way when he told him he didn't want to play ball and he wanted to go to college. Joey just sat there not realizing what was going on. Joshua told the kids that Rita and her children would be up at the end of the week to meet them. "That's so UN fair to drop another family off on us dad." Ebony cried and ran up to her room. Joshua was hurt by what Ebony said and hoped she wouldn't ruin it for the family by her spoiled attitude.

That weekend Rita arrived with Kara and Tommy. Joshua was introducing everyone the kids were staring each other down. Josh Jr. thought it might be cool to have another sister and little brother. Tommy was thinking and looking up at Josh Jr. and Joey and was beaming. "Wow, a big brother and a little brother." Joey likes the ideal of having another brother closer to his age. But the girls didn't feel the same. "Look at her looking at us like were aliens." Kara thought how Ebony was staring at them. "No daddy didn't just bring in these hillbilly's into our home, look at her she's fat and she ain't even cute, they'll laugh me out of school" Ebony said to her self. Then ran up stairs and slammed the door and called Tina. "Well that went well."

56

THE STEP FAMILY

Joshua said unfortunately to Rita who was disappointed the first meeting didn't go well at all. "Mother, daddy just brought some woman and her kids into our home, he says he wants to marry her, he can't do that mother!" Ebony cried. Tina was surprised that Joshua had been seeing someone else and now talking about marriage. Then she wondered about if it would affect her income being that she was already having a hard time now with Jack spending so much of it. "Let me speak to your father!" Tina said over the phone, when Tina got Joshua on the phone she went at him. "How dare you bring your new bitch and her brats into our home around the kids without preparing them!" Tina screamed "First this is my home and I know you ain't got the nerve to call me and talk about preparing anybody, you didn't prepare me or the kids when you started sleeping with your boy toy." Joshua blasted back. "Jack is not a boy toy and were not talking about him." "Then don't you go calling my lady or her children any foul names, now if we can talk adult like. I know our daughter has a problem with me moving on, so I'm hoping that you can talk to her and let her know, that we will never get back together, so she can let go that notion and face the fact." Joshua told her. "Fine but first I think we need to meet, so I'll host a party on Saturday, we can call it your engagement party." She said "Please Tina you're not going to throw us a party unless it's a lot of drama, no thank you." "Come on Joshua we have kids this way they will see we are still cordial to each other and this will help the kids handle this situation." "I have to talk it over with my fiancée and get back to you, bye Tina." Then Joshua hung up to go talk to Rita. "I think it will be okay, Joshua we all have to learn to get along for the sake of the children, this will be a start." Rita said thinking that it will be more helpful for Ebony who wouldn't even come down stairs for dinner. Rita kept her thoughts to her self, but if one of her kids acted like that she would of drug them down stairs and made them sit at the table and just look at the plate. Rita could see Joshua was having a hard time raising a teenage daughter especially a spoiled rude one.

After dinner Josh Jr. took Kara on a ride through the city to show her the sights. Joey and Tommy was inseparable since they met, Joey brought Tommy to his room and showed him all his toys. Tommy thought it was Christmas, never had he seen so many toys and Joey had all the late as ones. Rita and Joshua talked briefly about Joey being Jack's child but she knew it was a touchy incident for Joshua so she kept her opinions to herself, but loved the fact that Joshua was a good man and didn't split the kids up. Joshua and Rita were happy how most of the kids were getting alone. After cleaning up, they sat down in the living room on the couch to talk more about the marriage. "You know I love you Rita, and this will be my last year in the league, so if you want to wait until after I finish to get married I'll wait." Joshua told her. "If it's okay Joshua I've waited long enough for you to come into my life I would like to get married soon as possible." She smiled happily. "That's fine with me I'd only want to stay here while I finish playing and then we could all move back to Chicago so you can continue your work at the shop, I know you love it and don't want to

THE STEP FAMILY

ly, thank you, I worried about that the most, I love my shop and I love
'ta confessed. Joshua held her in his arms and thought how different
...s even with all his money she still was her own woman. Joshua wished now
that he could have seen all her qualities way back in high school, so many years he
missed with this beautiful woman.

Josh Jr. was driving Kara around the hip spots for the high school kids, all the
kids knew him as he drove his new black range rover. Everyone calling out JJ Jr.
"Wow, everyone knows you." Kara said surprised to see all the kids yelling his name.
"Yeah I'm JJ Jr. Joshua Jones son, and everyone wants to be my friend, you'll see
once you get in the family." He said. "Josh how do you feel about our parents getting
married?" "I think it's cool, dad was bumped out after him and my mother broke
up and she got a new boy friend, he needs somebody too, and your mother seems
like a nice woman." "Thanks, Josh she is and she deserves to be happy, my daddy
didn't do her right, but your father is so nice, how is it like being Joshua Jones son?"
"Honestly it's really hard people expect me to be like him a baller and between me
and you I don't even like the game." He said. "So why do you play it?" Kara asked
"because it makes dad happy and that's what he expects." "See my mama told me
to choose whatever I wanted to do, because if I'm gonna make my career doing it,
it should be something I want." "I wish my father thought like that." Josh said sadly.
"Talk to him he might surprise you." "Yes that would be a big surprise if he didn't
expect me to follow in his foot steps, anyway I like talking to you Kara, I think it's
going to be nice having a down to earth sister, because as you can see Ebony is so
spoiled and stuck up. And don't take it personal she doesn't like too many people."
Josh Jr. tried to explain. "I guess I'm one of those people she doesn't like." Kara said
sadly hoping for her mother that things would go good.

That night when they got back home, Rita had her room next to Joshua. Tommy
got to share a room with Joey who was overjoyed because these two boys had really
bonded. Josh Jr. went to his room and Kara got a room next to Ebony. As Kara
laid down in her bed she smiled thinking how nice it was to be staying in this big
mansion and her mama about to marry one of the most famous ball players ever,
and though they weren't poor, now her mama would never have to worry about
money. And long as she was happy that was the most important thing. Kara was
deep in thought and almost fell asleep when she heard a small knock on her door.
When Kara got up in open the door it was Ebony. Kara was happy thinking Ebony
had something nice to say. "Look, I just wanted to tell you that you and your family
are not welcome here and if you could talk to your mother and make her understand
that it wont be a marriage if I got anything to do with it." Ebony said with an angry
look on her face. "Why would you try to destroy your father's happiness?" Kara
asked "He don't want your fat mother when he could have my beautiful mother, he
just doesn't know it that's all." She blasted. "First that will be the first and last time

THE STEP FAMILY | 59

I better hear you talk about my mama, because if you do it again, I'm gonna have to hurt you. Second if you try to mess up their marriage I'm gonna hurt you, you spoiled stuck up brat!" Kara yelled "I am what I am, and yes my mother and father gives me everything that I want, so what!" Ebony yelled back "So why wont you let him have who he wants and let them be happy!" Kara yelled. "She just wants his money, he couldn't possibly love her." "Why couldn't he Ebony!" Kara yelled with her fist balled. "He couldn't because she is ghetto trash like you and your brother and you probably steal, so I will be locking my room up while you people are here and I hope it's not long!" Ebony yelled then went to her room. Kara stood there steaming mad. "I should go over there and yank that fake hair out of her head!" Kara said to her self then closed the door and went to bed.

The next morning at breakfast Joshua made Ebony come downstairs to eat with the family. Both girls sitting opposite from each other glaring at each other angrily. Joshua and Rita looked at them, and then each other wondering why these two girls looked like they wanted to get up and start fighting. "Ebony I'm glad you came down to eat with the family, everything will be great just wait and see." Joshua said "Dad you made me come down stairs but you can't make me like these people." Ebony yelled. "These people, you act like we are a bunch of niggers and your some white master of a plantation!" Kara yelled back. "Well I'm not white, but" then Ebony stopped in gave Kara a look like she was beneath her. "Mama, I'm sorry but I'm gonna hurt this girl if she says another thing about us!" Kara yelled "look you might be coming in the family but I can't let you go hurting my sister." Josh Jr. interjected. "I'm not scared of you JJ Jr. I'll take you on too!" Kara yelled, and then the three teenagers started arguing while the parents were trying to break it up. Joey started crying and the sweet as thing happen. Tommy sitting next to him hugged him and said "Your still my brother and wiped his eyes. Rita saw this and it brought her to tears. "Look at these babies there acting better than you so called grown teenagers. Joshua saw how Tommy was comforting Joey and he remembered how Ben was always there for him, and it gave him a strange feeling, how this boy that doesn't even know Joey can show him genuine love. Joshua was just going with the flow; still not able to accept this child as his son he was humbled. Rita then invited everyone to pray, Ebony was more upset now seeing the family trying to bond, ran up stairs to her room. The next few days went better Joshua loved Rita and the kids there and Kara and Josh Jr. made up. Tommy and Joey were always together and both boys were so happy to have each other. Ebony stayed out of every ones face still mad at everyone until the night of the engagement party because she knew her mama had something planned that would fix everything.

That night everyone got dressed up Joshua and Josh Jr. dressed in black suits while Rita and Kara had on two beautiful lavender dresses. Rita had fixed their hair and offered to fix Ebony's who had on a short sexy white dress responded to Rita

"You're not my mother!" Rita had to hold Kara back from attacking Ebony. Tina worked fast and got the party together in days and then called all the family. Joshua was shocked to see his parents the Rev and Mama Kelly there and as a surprise, Mama Kelly brought with them Anna and Glenda to Rita's delight, both of them was looking ghetto fabulist. The party was held at a huge convention center and it was decorated to the hilts. The place was packed along with the family a lot of Joshua's teammates and their wives were there. The couple and the kids got seated all together when Tina walked up to their table. Rita had seen pictures of Tina, but they didn't do her justice, Tina with her petite sexy look, she was beautiful having been fixed up to the max, hair, nails etc and her dress was a sexy black mini dress that looked like she was poured in it. Rita was not fat but she was full figured felt uneasy looking at Joshua beautiful ex wife. Tina smiled looking at Rita thinking that this woman didn't have anything on her. Tina made sure she looked extra good tonight to show everyone what Joshua left. Joshua introduced the two women, sensing Rita was feeling a little insecure he hugged her and kissed her on the fore head as he showed Tina he was happy and moved on. That's what Rita needed to bounce back. "Hello Tina, glad to meet you and thank you for throwing us this nice party and so short amount of time." Rita said "Oh I'm very efficient ask Joshua, and I'm glad to meet you also." Tina lied. "Well thanks again Tina and by the way where's Jack?" Joshua asked. Tina stood there now looking embarrassed, because at the last minute Jack decided not to come, because everyone knew he was a kept man. Before Tina could lie about Jack's where about, Ebony ran over to her and hugged her then Josh Jr. followed. "Where is Joey?" Tina asked. "We left him and Tommy Rita's son at the house with Dorothy." Joshua told her now starting to remember how they broke up and how he was put in the position of taking care of her child she had with Jack. "Well have a seat couple I have a lot of things planned for tonight, so enjoy this is your night." Tina said to them and as she walked away Ebony caught up with her. "Mother, what are you doing I wanted you to help break them up, why are you being so nice to that woman?" Ebony asked. "Don't worry, baby I got everything planned after tonight she'll run back to that hole she came from." Tina said smiling. The Rev and Mama Kelly and Glena and Anna were all seated with the family. Rita hugged Anna and Glenda and thanked them for coming. "Girl, I didn't come for you, I came to see if I can get me one of those country boys to take home." Anna said "Stop lying Anna you know we came to support our sister girl, you looking good girl and was that the ex you was talking to?" Glenda asked "yes, she's beautiful isn't she." Rita said "She might be a little cute, I don't like her white girl hair style, but as cute as she is, you got the man, so don't forget that, and you keep your head up." Glenda assured her. Rita smiled and felt better having her friends there and talking more with them and Joshua parents she was enjoying herself, then she looked over at Kara, who was sitting at the table looking, bothered. "What's the matter Kara, you're not enjoying the party?" Rita asked. "That's just it mama, some things not right, why would Joshua's ex wife want to do this for you and if she's anything like her daughter, I know some things up, so keep your guards up mama." Kara said nervous for her mother. Rita thanked her daughter and she could tell by Tina's face this wasn't genuine and she figured it was something else planned, but she hoped she was wrong.

So far the party was going good everyone ate lobster and shrimp and there was a great band that played, where people danced. Everyone laughed when Glenda took the floor and danced up a storm. "Where did that woman get her ghetto friends." Tina laughed to herself. Then before the party was over Tina got up front to say a few words. "I'd like to thank you all for coming to this party for Joshua and his fiancée. I'm sure they appreciate this especially Rita who probably isn't use to all this first class treatment, but she will be part of our family and I can't wait to take her around town and especially with me to my gym to work out." Tina said grinning everyone including the family was shocked. Ebony started laughing; Joshua looked at Tina with anger knowing she was trying to embarrass Rita. Kara had tears in her eyes she was so upset at this woman and Ebony. "Oh, no she didn't try to front my girl, she don't know me Anna she gonna have me coming down here getting a case!" Glenda told Anna who nodded just as upset. Rita had a feeling something was coming and she was embarrassed but she wasn't gonna let miss thing get away with this, so Rita got up cleared her throat and said. "Like my future husband EX wife said we thank you for coming, this was wonderful for my future husband EX wife to throw for us, don't you think?" Rita said then all the people was agreeing, Mama Kelly gave Rita a wink knowing Rita was just starting to pay Tina back for her crude remarks. "And I can't wait to start my life with this wonderful man" Rita said looking at Joshua who was grinning ear to ear and Tina was now livid. Then Rita continued. "Unfortunately Tina I won't be able to go around town or the gym with you because unlike you I have a job that I'm proud of. I'll be too busy working and taking care of this man and our children and being a FAITHFUL Christian wife, so like I said thanks again and can everyone give my Joshua's EX wife a hand for putting this on." Rita said then sat down, Glenda and Anna was slapping five, while the people clapped and yelled "You go girl!" Joshua stood up and went over and hugged Rita and thanks everyone for coming and told the crowd he was so happy now being with this wonderful woman and how he loved her kids. Kara wiped her eyes now loving this man who truly was a good man and a great father. Joshua then finished with "I'd like to thank my EX wife Tina also for throwing this party and to remember the only one that wants a bone is a dog." The whole room busted out laughing; everyone except Ebony and Tina who stood up in walked out. The party went on and everyone had a great time the rest of the night. On the way home Ebony started yelling at her father. "Dad why did you say those things to my mother and you!" Ebony said looking at Rita "You can never be the kind of lady my mother is." "Yes because my mother is a better one." Kara yelled back. "Stop it, both of you!" Rita yelled. "Kara you know better and Ebony I have to apologize to you,

I should not of fell into that trap your mother set up and I really feel now that we both embarrassed each other. We can't start this family like this; we have to learn how to get along." Rita said. "I'll never accept you into my life, I have a mother." Ebony cried. "No ones trying to take that from you baby, we know you love your mother and that's wonderful, but our marriage is over, been over and I have Rita now. Tonight your mother tried to embarrassed Rita but she got the tables turned on her, and Rita I'm so proud of you how you stood your ground and like you I can't wait to marry you, so let's move up the date." Joshua said. Rita smiled and hugged her husband to be. Kara had tears of joy sitting next to her new brother Josh Jr. Josh who sat back watching everything and like Ebony he loved his mother, but what she tried to do tonight wasn't right. And he also noticed that Jack wasn't there like usual. Josh Jr. knew his father had to move on and this lady was good for him and Kara and Tommy were good kids who even after only a few days was considering them family. Ebony unfortunately was hurting; she sat in the corner of the limo feeling like everyone was against her. Rita saw the unhappiness in this young girl and wanted to help, but Ebony had to let her in, but Rita wasn't going to let her spoil what would be wonderful for her and her children a husband and a father.

After a few more days it was time for Rita and her children to go back home. Joey and Tommy did a lot of crying when Rita and the kids had to go back to Chicago. The parents finally convinced the two boys they would all be back together soon, but when it was time to get on the plane to go home it was a lot of teary eyes. "I'm gonna miss you baby, I feel like your part of me now." Joshua said holding onto his fiancée. Tears in her eyes Rita hugged him back and told him she couldn't wait to marry him so she would never have to leave again.

CHAPTER NINE

YOU MADE YOUR BED SO LAY IN IT

THE NEXT FEW weeks were hard Joshua was traveling all over playing ball. This year they had a better team, the team drafted some new members one was this eighteen year old, six foot eight skinny light skin new forward, who was called the next Joshua Jones his name was Flex Spencer. Joshua thought it was funny how the media already retired him and chose somebody to take his place, but so far now at thirty eight years of age and twenty years of playing and still no championship ring. That bothered Joshua but now he was going to be married and retire, but he did want to go out a champion and a MVP would be good also but mostly he wanted his team to win.

Joshua being the team captain went over to welcome Flex to the team but was surprised at his arrogant. "Look old man they ain't put you out to pastured yet, well I'm the new sheriff in town that's gonna help us get that ring this year." Flex smirked. Joshua was surprised at how this boy that was the same age as his son was so disrespectful. Joshua knew it was time to leave. "What ever it takes hot head, but remember where a team." "That was before I got here, you just keep passing the ball to me and I'll help you go out a winner instead of being losers all these years." Flex said with disgust. Joshua looked at him with shock and was glad that the rest of the team didn't hear that crap. To Joshua delight Roy, Ebony's boy friend was drafted also to their team. This would be a good time to bond more with this kid and see if he could some how help Ebony come to terms with his up coming wedding and just thinking of Rita brought a smile to his face.

"Ladies here comes the ballers wife." Glenda yelled to the rest of the shop when Rita walked in the door late. "I'm sorry, I'm late I was up all night planning the wedding an over slept, is my client here yet?" Rita asked. "No, she's late too you colored people always late." Glenda laughed "No you didn't Glenda you blacker than a black hole!" Anna said and laughed back. "Girl I ain't mad, that's why they call me black berry at the clubs." Glenda smiled. "You two are something else, I need to talk to you two in the back for a minute." Rita asked. When they all entered the back office Rita started off saying "I need a favor from you two, you know I'm getting married and plan on moving to Houston to stay with Joshua his last season then come back after he's done, so I'm gonna have to leave the shop." Both Glena and Anna were looking at each other sadly about the loss of their jobs until Rita continued and said. "I want you two to keep the shop going until I get back and if your willing to do this I will make you part owners of the shop, what do you say?" Rita asked hoping they wanted the responsibility of owning a shop. Both Anna and Glena were jumping up in down yelling. "Girl, don't do that, I thought we was getting a pink slip, this is wonderful, I would love to hold it down for you and be a partner." Anna expressed. "Me too, I just can't wait to put my touch on this place to brighten this shop, I mean our shop up." Glenda said, and then all three of them had a group hug and went back to work.

Now most everyone was happy for the couples in coming marriage except for a few, Tina was one. Tina walked through out her lonely home still feeling the shame of how she got blasted at the party and how she could even try to hurt Joshua. Tina had to admit he was only good to her and when she married Joshua she wanted to be rich and have nice things and she had all that she wanted to make her happy. Tina had the big house cars, jewelry and she didn't have to work, and Joshua was taking care of the kids so she wasn't tied down behind that. Most important she had Jack the love of her life, only thing he was running through all her money like water, but she loved him. Jack was so fine and he made her feel so good that it was hard to say no to him. Tina heard about women that put their men before everything even their kids, but she never thought she would be one of them. It was twelve am and Jack wasn't home and wouldn't answer his page. Tina waited up knowing Jack was going to come home and lie and say he was at a male friends house, instead of a woman house where she suspected he was at. Tina wasn't stupid she could sense he was messing around he wasn't given it to her as much and was gone a lot. While Tina laid in bed waiting her phone rang.

"Who is this?" the lady asked. "Who is this, you called my phone." Tina said getting angry. "Well I'm Jack's lady and he forgot his phone tonight and I wanted to know who keeps calling him!" she yelled. "My name is Tina and I'm Jack's woman, the woman he's living with, again who are you and how long have you

THE STEP FAMILY   65

been thinking you was his lady?" Tina asked upset. "My name is Wendy Talbot and me and Jack has been together for two years and we have a one year old son!" The lady yelled. Tina dropped the phone in shock, shaking she picked it up and turned it off. Ten minutes later Jack walked in the dark bedroom and tried to sneak in bed without Tina hearing him thinking she was asleep when he got in. Tina turned on her lamp; Jack turned in saw her eyes all red from crying. "Where have you been Jack?" she asked wiping her eyes. "I was out with the boys, go back to sleep" he said. "I was trying to sleep before I got a phone call from some woman named Wendy she says you left your phone there and she was wondering why I was calling you." "That's just a friend, nothing serious I must of dropped my phone and she picked it up" he lied. "Nothing serious, she says she has a one year old son by you, tell me your not having more kids when you wont even claim Joey the one you already have, tell me Jack!" Tina yelled. "Look Tina I tell you what you want to hear, I do what you want done that's take care of you emotionally and physically, now if you want to change the rules of this game. I'll just get out of this bed and leave!" Jack yelled and then got up ready to go out the door "Wait, wait don't go I don't want to lose you Jack I love you." Tina said sadly. "Fine, I'll stay but no more talk of that woman!" then Jack got back in bed and began doing what he did best and that was taking care of her physically. Tina laid there thinking what a fool she had become.

Days later back in Chicago Rita was at the church getting it ready for the wedding when she had a visitor walk behind her and tap her on her shoulder. "Hello Rita long time no see, you're looking good." Rita who had been losing weight to get into her wedding gown turned around in saw Matt standing there. "Matt what brings you here?" Rita asked shocked. "I heard about your wedding and wanted to see you and the kids" he said looking sad. Rita heard how he and Mildred was living in some old trailer park and how little pretty Miss Thang wasn't little anymore. Mildred had gain so much weight that she was now bigger than Rita and Rita wasn't going to throw that in his face because of the way he did her. Rita had moved on and if she was still with Matt she would not be marring Joshua, knowing God has his reason, but she knew Matt had another reason for the visit. "Matt please what do you want I know it's not the kids you haven't came around in years and even though I'm not asking for child support you could of at least gave the kids Christmas or birthday gifts or at least call, but you've done nothing and now you come, why?" Rita asked knowing it was more to his visit. "Look Rita, I've had bad times me and Mildred, you know she doesn't work, so I had to go back to dumping garbage to survive, but we got so many bills and I was wondering since your marring Joshua, and he's rich you can help me out" he begged. "Matt, tell me why would I want to do that. You remember you left me, cheated on me, you left our children and you have the nerve to come in my face in ask for handouts. Why would you think I'd want to help you,

you have not even given me anything for the kids" Rita said shocked. "Why because I was married to you and we have kids and your suppose to be a Christian woman and you don't want me going back to court to try to get custody of our kids" he said ashamed but desperate. "Look Matt you do what you need to do, all I know is that you got out of my bed to go lay in another, so you go back in lay in it, I'll see you in court!" Rita yelled. Matt walked away knowing he couldn't go to court, no way would a judge give him the kids over Rita and now Joshua. Matt could hardly afford to take care of him and Mildred, no way could he take care of his kids if Rita didn't give him any money. Plus Matt couldn't do that to his children and have them stuck in a trailer, but he needed the money so he thought he try. What bothered him the most now was how he uses to get angry how Joshua had all the girls after him and now years later he's marring the woman he already had. That night Rita called Joshua and told him about what happen. Joshua laughed and said. "Baby it seems like our Ex's wasn't happy when they were with us but now they want to start all this drama. Maybe we ought to introduce Matt to Tina, and then they could hook up and leave us alone" he laughed. "I won't let anyone ruin our marriage speaking of trouble how's Ebony?" Rita asked. "She's upstairs still mad, but I do have someone standing next to me that wants to talk to his brother." Joshua smiled as Joey kept pulling at his arm so he could talk to Tommy.

Day's later Ebony came running in the house crying. Josh Jr. was at the kitchen table when he heard her come in then ran up the stairs. "Dad something's wrong with Ebony" Josh Jr. told his father. Joshua was sitting outside by the pool reading the paper, jumped up then they both went up stairs to Ebony's room, who wouldn't open the door or talk to them so Joshua called Tina. "What am I suppose to do Joshua you got the kids, I got problems of my own, why don't you call your new wife!" Tina yelled. "Look Tina, that's your daughter up there hurting and you got just what you deserved, your lucky Rita didn't slap the mess out of you for playing that trick on us, that's over now and Ebony needs her mother. So do your job damn it!" Joshua yelled. An hour later Tina got to the house and hugged Josh Jr. and Joey who was happy to see her then went up stairs and knocked on the door and told Ebony to let her in. Ebony ran to the door open it and saw her mother then jumped into her arms crying. "What's wrong Ebony?" Tina asked scared for her daughter. Ebony and Tina sat on the bed and Ebony wiped her eyes and said. "Roy dumped me, he said I was too spoiled and he didn't want to start his career being held down with all my drama!" Ebony cried. Tina held her daughter and told her it was going to be all right, but she knew Ebony was just like her a rich spoiled little girl, but Tina was lucky she got her jock, but Ebony didn't and now she was in pain. After an hour Tina came down stairs and told Joshua what had happen and told him that he should some how get Roy kicked off the team for hurting their daughter. "Tina I wouldn't if I could, Roy is right, Ebony is spoiled rotten, that's our fault and I cant

THE STEP FAMILY | 67

blame him for not wanting to get locked up in drama, he's just lucky he's getting out before." Then Joshua stopped talking. "Before what Joshua, before he has kids, like us, is that what your trying to say!" "No Tina, I love my kids and you know that I'm even taking care of your boy friends child, but our marriage was a mistake the kids weren't, now thank you for coming, but now I have to turn in we got a game tomorrow" he said. "And you'll be getting married Saturday, I didn't get my invitation Joshua" she said. "That's because we didn't send it, after that stunt you pulled at our party, I would not be able or want to stop her friends from hurting you if you came to our wedding and caused any problems. Rita got some crazy friends that would surly deal with you" Joshua said. Tina got up in walked out the door thinking. "He knows I wouldn't of came anyway" she said to herself.

The day of the wedding it was a sunny Saturday in Chicago. The church was decorated in white and pink, the choir had sung a few songs while the guest entered the church and sat down on the chairs that were all covered with pink and white flowers. Rita didn't want it to be too fancy because this was both their second marriage and it was at church. The church was packed with friends and family. Anna and Glenda was there of course, they both helped with the hairstyles. Donta and Lewis were there also to support their boy. This wedding was a family affair, so it started with Ben, Joshua's brother marring the couple, as he stood at the front of the church proud of his brother Joshua and honored that Joshua wanted him to perform the wedding. Joshua was thrilled that Josh Jr. both dressed in white tuxes was his best man and walked him up to the arch where Ben was. Then came Tommy to light the candles, he walked up there all smiles in his white tux. Anna's little girl was the flower girl who threw the pink flower peddles through out the church. Then came Joey all suited up in his little white Tux caring the rings he was so happy. Joshua wondered how he was going to take it one day when he learns that he isn't really his father, before Joshua could finish his thought, up came walking in her beautiful pink dress was Kara. Rita wanted Ebony to be a bride maid, but she didn't want to come and Joshua thought it might be better for her to stay home with her mother, than to come down in ruin the wedding. Joshua wished that Ebony could feel like Kara who was so happy for her mother. After Kara took her place everyone stood up while The Rev walked Rita in. Mama Kelly was sitting up front, getting all misty watching all her family so happy. Rita had on a beautiful creamy white dress that had a high collar and long sleeves and pink rhinestones in front. Her hair was laid down then flipped back, her make up was flawless, all done by Glenda who was an expert on make up and hair. Rita wanted to pinch herself as she walked up to greet her husband to be. Rita had to hold back her laughter when she thought how she had this man's pictures on her wall when she was younger now she was marring him. Joshua was wondering how he could have overlooked this wonderful lady all through church and school. When Ben asked who was giving Rita away and The

Rev said "I am." It took all Rita could to hold back the tears how The Rev took the place for a father she never had and a mother that had died. The wedding went off without a hitch. Everything was beautiful.

Later everyone went to The Rev house for the reception; Mama Kelly out did her self with all the food she had for the guest. "Rita the wedding was beautiful but what I want to know is what you got planned for your honeymoon?" Glenda asked. "Were going to cruise to the Bahamas again, later after this season. That way we can stay as long as we want, but for now, we'll just go back to my home and then we'll, all fly back to Joshua home before the next game. "Yes and Kara and Tommy are staying with me this weekend and Josh Jr. and Joey are staying here with The Rev, so you two can blow that house up!" Anna laughed. Rita laughed thinking how nice friends she has Anna and Glenda and now her new family, Joshua and his boys and even Ebony that she promised herself that she was gonna get that girl to come around.

That night Joshua carried Rita into her house and when they got in they both saw how someone had a trail of rose peddles going up to the bedroom. On the bed it was covered with more rose pedals, there was scented candles lit sending off a sweet aroma. The bathtub was filled and heated with bubbles, there was glasses and a bottle of Champaign and chocolate cherries and more candles lit around the tub. The lights were very dim in the bedroom and there was a Teddy Pendergrass song playing. "Wow, who could have done all this?" Joshua asked shocked but pleased. "Glenda, this looks like his work, he's such a freak, but I love him" Rita laughed. "You know Rita you got good friends and your kids are wonderful and they all love you because you're a beautiful person and I feel honored that you let me be your husband" Joshua said. Rita overwhelmed by all this love being shown to her, couldn't help wanting to thank God for all he had done for her. Rita asked Joshua it she could have a moment to pray and he said the most beautiful thing. "If I can pray with you" he said. Both of them feeling bless got on their knees and prayed and thanked God for this day and for the rest of their lives and to watch over their marriage and their family. That night they laid in each other arms and went to sleep, but the next morning it was on. The couple was ready to go to the next level as they laid there making love to each other. Joshua held on to his wife feeling so wonderful, this woman was bringing it home, he had a hard time not releasing, wanting to fully satisfy his wife. Rita's head was spinning thinking "Wow this man is so good I may never want to get out of bed." Never had either one of them experienced this complete joy. After hours of pure delight, "Girl, you got me so tired, I don't think I'll be able to walk, you wore me out!" Joshua sighed wiping the sweat off his forehead. "I can say you weren't so bad yourself, your soldier sure came out for duty!" Rita laughed. Joshua laughed also and told Rita how he couldn't wait to have everyone together as a family. "Yes husband, wow I like the sound of that, husband, "IAS married now" Rita said the line from the movie color purple, that brought both of them laughing again. The couple had the best weekend of their lives. That Monday the Rev and Mama Kelly, Ben and his family along with Glenda and Anna were all at the airport to see Rita and Kara and Tommy off with Joshua and Josh Jr. and Joey. All together they left as one family.

CHAPTER TEN

HOME IS WHERE THE HEART IS

THE NEW FAMILY flew back to Houston to their new lives. When they got home Dorothy was there to greet them. "Where's Ebony?" Joshua asked. "She's upstairs she got home today, and she's been in her room all day" Dorothy told him. Joshua went up stairs to talk to her. "Hi baby were all back" Joshua said happily. Ebony was lying across her bed with her headphone on listening to music. "Did you bring the step family back with you?" She asked. "No, I brought our family back and I'm hoping that you can try to get along with everyone, and how was your time with your mother?" he asked. "Terrible I rarely saw her and that man Jack; I don't like how he looks at me. "Did he say or do anything that I need to be concerned about?" Joshua asked. "No, he's lazy and sits around all day doing nothing while mother's a slave to him, then at night he leaves, sometimes she goes with him. Then the other times she's up in her room calling him. I just stayed in my room mostly, like I'll be doing here staying away from all of you!" Ebony said annoyed. "Why must you make this hard on everyone, for me I hope you will try to get along. If you let them you'll find out their good people." Joshua explained. Ebony just turned her back in put her earphone back on. Joshua shook his head in walked down stairs determined to not let Ebony ruin it for everyone. That night everyone got settled. Joey and Tommy had their room together; Kara got her big bedroom by Ebony. Rita was lying in her bed next to her new husband. After hearing about Ebony, Rita told Joshua that they just had to keep praying that she would come along.

THE STEP FAMILY

71

The next day every one except Ebony went to the stadium to watch Joshua play. Joshua's team was playing against the Portland Trail Blazers. Rita and the kids Josh Jr., Kara, Tommy and Joey was all up in the stands yelling for Joshua, who was having his best game in years. Joshua was always good but he started off great, then as time went on and problems occurred in his life he didn't play with his full potential. Now that he had his life on track, he was averaging thirty points a game, a long with Flex who scored in the top twenties and Roy averaging twenty points a game. Their team was the team to beat. Roy and Joshua played good together, but no matter what Joshua said Flex was still a ball hog. Flex wouldn't pass the ball if he got it and it was a huge problem with the team, but because the team was winning and wanting that ring, most of the team kept their disapproval to themselves. To nights game was like the last few Joshua team blew the other team away, especially on their home court, they were UN beatable. Josh Jr. watched the game and admired how his father was so good at it, because he loved it. Too bad Josh Jr. didn't, and then Rita asked him the question he dreaded. "JJ when do you plan on getting in the big league or are you going to college?" Rita asked, Josh Jr. was staring out in space not knowing what to say, until Kara poked him in his side and told him to tell her. "Tell me what?" Rita asked. "This is not the place Kara." "Sure it is Joey and Tommy aren't listening, they're into the game; tell mama how you feel Josh." "Josh, I know I'm not your mother, but I do care and you can tell me anything" Rita said. Josh Jr. thought how nice it was for someone to finally ask him how he felt and what he wanted, instead of like his father and mother continually pushing him into the game. "Rita honestly I don't like the game, I want to go to college and study to be a teacher." He said. "Then that's what you need to do and you ought to first tell your father. I'm sure he'll understand" Rita said. "Will you be there with me." "Sure son" "thanks mom" he said. That brought a smile to both Rita and Kara face. After winning the game Joshua took his family out to eat Kara and Rita felt like celebrities how everyone was yelling out Joshua's name and telling him how good the game was. Rita almost forgot how successful her new husband was.

Later Joshua was sitting in the den with Rita when Josh Jr. came in and asked if he could talk to him. "Sure son, what's the problem you look worried, what's up?" he asked. Josh Jr. looked over at Rita who nodded her head and said "tell him." "Tell me what, you got some girl pregnant, what is it!" Joshua said starting to get nervous. "No daddy I'm using rubbers everytime, I just wanted to tell you that." Then he stopped and looked at the floor. "Tell me what!" Joshua yelled. "Baby, Josh doesn't want to play basketball he wants to go to college and study to be a teacher, that's all." Rita blurted out trying to calm the situation. Joshua looked at his son with his head still down. "Son, why didn't you tell me, you can do what ever you want to do, you don't have to play ball if you don't want to. Why would you think you had to?" Joshua asked. "Because that's what I thought you and mom wanted me to do, and I wanted to make you happy and proud." He said. "You being happy makes me happy, you being a good son makes me proud and I love you son." Joshua said with tears in his eyes. Both men hugged then Josh went over in hugged Rita tight and cried in her arms feeling so relieved that this woman helped him finally come to terms with this problem. Joshua was overwhelmed watching Rita console his son, "Now you got to tell your mama." Joshua said.

"How dare you! Interfere with my family, that's my son and he needs to play ball like his father, so you need to keep you nose out of our business!" Tina yelled at Rita over the phone after talking to her son. "First I don't appreciate your tone and second Josh Jr. doesn't want to play ball, and he's old enough to make his own decision with his life, don't you think." Rita told her starting to heat up. "No, I think you want my son to be poor like you and your trailer trash family!" Tina screamed. "Tina you better be glad that I'm saved and your not here because you would be testing my religion right now. Josh wants to work hard like I have been doing since I was a small girl. I've always been able to feed my family and kept a roof over their heads and now don't forget and you know better than anyone that I have a very rich husband now. Thank you very much and goodbye!" Rita said and hung up the phone. That night when Rita told Joshua what Tina had said Joshua wanted to call Tina up in cuss her out, but Rita told him to let it go and not let her disrupt their family.

The next day Joshua and Rita enrolled Kara into the Truman High school a private school were the rich kids went to. Josh Jr. was a senior now, Ebony was a sophomore and Kara was a junior. Soon as they all got to school, Ebony left in went to class. Josh showed Kara all around school and introduced her to all of the kids. They loved her down to earth manner. Unfortunately Ebony was having a harder time now because she didn't have many friends. Most of all the kids were filthy rich too so they couldn't understand how Ebony walked around thinking she was better than everyone else. The girls would make fun of her and called her a dumb blond, because of her grades, so she had to deal with that and now her so called stepsister. "Why are you showing that trash around our school!" Ebony yelled at Josh in the hallway. "Ebony stop hating, Kara's cool, if you get to know her, you always said you wished you had a sister." Josh said. "That tramp will never be my sister!" Ebony screamed. Josh shook his head in walked away. Ebony stood there ready to cry, she loved her brothers Josh and Joey so much and she did wish she had a sister, but she also wanted her father and mother back together and Rita and her family was in the way.

While Ebony stood there hurting Denise Dawn a dark over weight senior in her posse of girls walked over and shoved Ebony to the ground. Denise hated Ebony

THE STEP FAMILY | 73

because she was beautiful in spoiled. "Get up pretty girl, so I can knock you down again, oh wait I heard Roy dumped your ass, I guess you ain't as pretty as you think." Denise laughed along with the rest of the girls. "Denise I flushed stuff out of me that looked better than you." Ebony yelled back, still on the ground. "Ebony you're just like your spoil ass cheating mama!" Denise yelled. "Don't you talk about my mother!" Ebony yelled in got up in charged Denise. Denise grabbed her in threw her against the wall, then one of the girls told Denise a teacher was coming that way. "Next time I catch you bitch I'm kicking your ass!" Denise yelled then walked away with her crew. Ebony rubbed her bruises and went to class, knowing she couldn't tell in be called a snitch but she knew the next time she might not be so lucky.

That night the family was all together talking over the day. Joshua told the family that he was going to have to travel and play five games on the road and they had made the play off. Rita and Josh Jr. and Kara were all hoping this would be the year that they won the championship. Meanwhile Tommy and Joey were playing in their room when Joey told Tommy that Ebony had a video game that he wanted to play. So Tommy noticed how Ebony didn't say much but was too young to understand the hatred she had for them, so he didn't think twice to knock on Ebony's door to see if he could borrow the game. Ebony was lying on her bed with her ear phones on so she didn't hear him knocking on the door, so after a while Tommy open the door and went in and saw her. Ebony was still upset at what happen at school so she was not in the mood, so when she saw Tommy she yelled. "Get out of my room, you little bastard!" Tommy ran out the room scared then went back to his room and cried. Joey put his arm around his brother in patted him on the back to try to make him stop crying when it didn't work he walked down stairs and Kara saw him first with tears in his eyes "what's wrong Joey?" Kara asked concerned. "Tommy is sad, he's crying." "Why what happen?" she asked. "He went into Ebony's room for a game and she got mad." He cried "Oh no she didn't!" Kara said storming mad. This time Ebony went too far when Kara went to see about Tommy he told her that Ebony hates him and called him a bastard. "Am I a bastard, Kara I thought I was just a little boy" he cried. "You are a sweet, good little boy, and don't let anybody tell you different." "Yes Tommy, I like you." Joey said warming Kara's heart but not enough to stop her from busting into Ebony's room. "What are you doing in my room, get out, what's wrong with you people!" Ebony yelled. "Why did you call my brother a bastard!" Kara yelled upset. "Because he walked in my room, like you without permission!" "He's just a little boy, Ebony your out of line." "So what if I am, if you don't like it, leave and take him and your money grubbing mother too!" "I think you must be talking about your mama, she's the one with the money problems." Kara said. After today that was enough Ebony lost it and went after Kara, swinging and yelling, Kara just threw her down on the floor and jumped on her. Ebony was yelling so loud that Joey and Tommy ran downstairs and got the rest of the family. Joshua got up stairs first and pulled Kara off of Ebony. "What's going on in here!"

he yelled. "Kara you know better than this what's wrong with you!" Rita shouted at her. "That evil girl called Tommy a bastard and she called you a money grubber and that's not the first time she said bad things about you mama." Kara tried to explain. "Kara that's okay Ebony just trying to adjust to us" Rita said. "No baby that's not okay, Ebony why are you saying bad things about your family?" Joshua asked upset. "Step family and she talked about my mother, I hate them why can't they just leave!" Ebony cried. "Ebony after this season I am going home to Chicago with our new family and I plan on taking all of you with me," Joshua expressed. "I'm not going and Josh Jr. I know you don't want to leave?" Ebony asked. "Sure I do, sis I'm gonna go with my family and I hope you will go too." He said. "But what about mother?" she asked. Josh got quiet then looked at Ebony and said "Ebony she left us a long time ago, plus she has Jack, we can come back to visit." Josh explained. "I'm not leaving my mother and I'm not staying in this house another minute, dad your always sticking up for them, I want to go stay with my mother!" Ebony demanded. "Ebony I'm sorry you feel that way about us, but if you just give us a chance to make things better." Rita asked. "No Rita, let her go, but Ebony we will always be here for you." Joshua said.

Ebony packed her bags and Josh Jr. drove her to her mother's home who was shocked to see her daughter and with all her thing. "What's going on Ebony?" Tina asked. "Mother I couldn't take it anymore there I had to get out, I came here to stay." "Fine Ebony take your stuff to your room." Tina said feeling upset that now her life is going to change now that her pretty daughter will be walking around the house and Tina was already having problems with Jack in his womanizing. That night lying in bed Rita told Joshua how sorry she was about how Ebony left. "Baby, don't be sorry what family don't have problems we just got to be strong and hold on. Ebony never really got over me and her mother breaking up, but let her stay over there with her mama for a while then she will come running back." Joshua said.

The next morning when Ebony got up for school, no one was up, both Tina and Jack was still in the bed. Every time her father was home he was up in the morning when she got up to have breakfast with the kids, then if Josh Jr. didn't drive her to school her father would. The only ones that were up for Ebony were the maid and the cook, two Hispanic ladies that was told by Tina to speak only when spoken to. So Ebony called Josh Jr. to come over and pick her up for school. When he got there Kara was in the car, so Ebony got in the back and the three of them road to school in silence. When they got to the school Ebony jumped out the car in went in, not saying a word. Josh shook his head feeling sorry for his sister and after a long conversation with Rita, Kara was also. Rita told Kara that Ebony was hurting; her life had been changed, when her mother and father had broken up. Tina had grew up spoiled getting every thing she wanted thinking all you got to do is look pretty, but that's not real and Tina taught Ebony the same thing so she doesn't

THE STEP FAMILY

know better, so pray for her. Kara thought about it and when her father left her mother she was angry too, but she had to let go and let God work it out. And now her mama was happy married to a wonderful man and she had two new brothers and she was hoping to have a sister, but it wasn't working out very well. Weeks pass with the three teenagers still riding to school together and Ebony not talking to anyone. Josh and Kara stopped expecting Ebony to join in the conversations, they would have as they rode to school, and Ebony would just sit in the back and pout. Then one day Josh mention how since he quit playing ball he loss all his girl friends and Kara joked "from what I heard you didn't play good anyway" and from the back they heard Ebony chuckle. Both Josh and Kara winked at each other hoping maybe, this was a start.

On the court the play off had started and so far it was only Houston and New York left. The first game was to be held in Houston and the two team's record was about the same, because Houston had slipped some and suffered some losses due to Flex, not wanting to be on the team anymore and the team not wanting to play with him. So no one wanted to pass him the ball and when he did get it, it was all about him. Flex wanted to be traded to LA or New York. Joshua tried to talk to Flex and explain to him it was hard for them to win if they didn't play as a team and they were so close to getting the ring. "Look old man, sure I want the ring, but if I don't, I'll be able to play more, your team doesn't want me here and I don't want to be here!" "Flex, I don't have time, this is my last shot, and we can win this if we play together." "Yeah and you want to go out on top, but I'm the star here, but your teammates wont pass me the ball. So I want out, and I think you ought to be talking to them. Not me." Flex said in walked out. Joshua thought why after all these years and now finally getting so close to winning the championship that now he's stuck with a hot head, and was glad this would be his last season and he could go back home with his family and hoping his daughter would come also.

CHAPTER ELEVEN

DON'T BE A PICTURE BE A PERSON

EBONY WAS REALLY having a hard time staying at home with her mother. It was awful she didn't have Roy anymore and she found out he was dating another girl. Then being separated from her father and brothers and to top all that Denise was still walking around school wanting to beat her up. And because of that the few friends she had didn't want to hang around her and get beat up by Denise the school bully. Ebony tried to stay away from Denise as much as possible but one day while Ebony was in the gym with the other girls the gym teacher walked out the gym. Then one of the girls locked the door and Denise made her move. Denise and her gang approached Ebony, who was sitting in the corner of the room. "Now I got you bitch and you can't run!" Denise yelled with her fist out, and from the locker room all the girls started running out. Kara was in the locker room getting dressed and asked what was going on. "That bitch Ebony is finally gonna get hers, Denise is gonna beat her ass." One of the girls said. Kara not even thinking about it ran out to the gym and over the course of weeks, everyone grew to like Kara's down to earth attitude. Kara had no enemies until today, when she ran into the gym Denise had just shoved Ebony into the wall hard. Ebony knew she was going to get beat up, she didn't know how to fight all she knew was how to look pretty which wasn't going to do her any good now. Ebony knew no one was going to help her, so she stood there ready to get beat down, until by her surprise Kara walked up in stood in front of her. "What's up Denise, we got a problem!" Kara said looking straight in her eyes. "No, we don't Kara, just move out the way so I can take down pretty girl!" Denise said "No, I don't think so, that's my sister!" "What!" Ebony thought to her

THE STEP FAMILY

self, shocked surprised and overwhelm that Kara was sticking up for her and called her sister after all she had said to her, that brought tears to Ebony's eyes. "I think if you don't want the same thing I'm gonna do to Ebony, you had better get out the way!" Denise yelled. "Girl friend you don't know me. I'm not scared of you I lived in a neighborhood where we had to dodge bullets. So you don't scare me but I know you better back off with the quickness or I'm gonna show you how we roll back where I come from!" Kara said walking toward her with her fist balled and she could see the fear in Denise and her friends eyes as they backed off scared. Then the teacher came busting in with the security. "What's going on here!" The teacher asked upset. Then one of Denise's crew said that Kara was trying to beat them up. "No! Mrs. Green Denise was going to beat me up and my sister saved me!" Ebony explained. And to hear Ebony call her sister was worth the punishment she was about to get. Kara and Denise were both suspended for three days.

On the ride home Kara and Josh had little conversation while Ebony was sitting in the back still overwhelmed how this girl stuck up for her after she was so mean to her and her family. When Josh stopped the car at his mother's house Ebony got out the car and said thank you to Kara and then went into the house. "What's she thanking you for?" Josh asked "She's thanking me for saving her from a beat down today." Then Kara told Josh the whole story, Josh laughed all the way home, but Rita wasn't laughing, having got the phone call from the school. Joshua had came home and she told him about Kara being suspended. Rita was so mad she told Joshua that she wanted to borrow one of his belts. "Baby you cant beat the girl, she's too old, but then maybe if I would have whooped Ebony's butt, she might have not been so spoiled." Joshua said. Then Kara and Josh Jr. walked in the house and Kara saw the look on her mama's face. "Wait mama before you ground me, let me explain." Kara begged. "Girl it better be good, because you know I raised you better than this!" Rita said waiting for an explanation. "Mom, Ebony was gonna get beat up by this girl at school in Kara stuck up for her." Josh said trying to help his sister. Both Joshua and Rita eyes grew wide shocked that Kara would stand up for Ebony after all that went on. "Okay Miss Ali, no phone for one day." Rita said. "Thanks mama, oh I mean okay mama." Kara said knowing she just got let off the hook and didn't want to sound too happy about it. After her and Josh went upstairs both parents had tears in their eyes. "I think we might make it." Joshua said so overwhelmed by his family. Meanwhile when Ebony got home she overheard her mother and Jack arguing.

"Jack that woman called again, do you take me for some kind of a fool. You can't keep treating me like this or." "Or what, I'm treating you like you want, and no I don't take you for a fool but a rich little spoiled woman that never had to do a days work in your life." "I know your not talking about work, since we've been together you never had a job!" "Tina I do work, my job is to take care of you and my tool is in my pants, and you pay me well." "Well you know that makes you a hoe." "Yes, my love in that would make you my trick." He said and walked out in saw Ebony at the door. "What's the matter baby girl, don't like what you see, you will, your just like your mama and you'll end up with a man just like me." He said in walked out the door. Ebony was so sick at the thought she felt like throwing up. "Mother, why do you let him treat you like that?" Ebony asked. "Because I love him and he's the only man I've ever loved." Tina said. "What about daddy?" Ebony asked shocked. "Grow up child, he wanted a pretty girl, and I wanted a rich husband. You see Ebony after I left my rich parent's I did what my mother wanted me to do find a rich man, so I'd always have the finer things in life. So I did and got married to your rich father and it all worked out, until my heart took control. Now I have money and a man that I love, everything turned out good." Tina said trying to convince herself and Ebony that everything was fine. "If it's so good mother, than why aren't you happy?" Ebony asked sadly thinking this is the kind of life she wants her to have.

The next few days at school no one bothered Ebony to her delight. On one of the ride home from school Josh and Ebony talked about their new family. "I told you Kara was cool and Tommy he loves Joey so much. You should see those two, Tommy he shows Joey how to read, and it does something to your heart to see Joey looking out the window waiting for Tommy to come home, he don't even do that for dad. Ebony you know you should really apologize to Tommy and Rita, she's made for dad. I have never seen him so happy and that's what we want him and mother happy even though we both know that Jack's a jerk." Josh said "Jack's a big time jerk, he got mother's head all messed up, I can't go out like that." Ebony said. "Then maybe you ought to come with us after dad gets done with the play off. I know he wants you to come and Joey does too, and you know I want you with us sis." Josh told her. Ebony rode the rest of the way thinking about what Josh had said and how hard it would be for her with them gone.

The next morning Josh came to the house to pick up Ebony for school and Kara was in the car, done with her suspension. Ebony got in the back seat, but didn't say much still shamed of how she treated Kara. Then at lunch time Kara walked in the lunchroom in got her food and saw Ebony in the corner sitting by her self-eating her lunch. "I know she doesn't like me, but at lease she don't hate me anymore, maybe I can sit at her table." Kara said to her self. When Ebony looked up, she was shocked to see someone coming to sit with her and saw it was Kara. Both girls sat there eating quietly until Ebony said. "I like your hair, you always have the best styles." "That's cause mama does my hair, that's what she does." Kara said surprised to be having a civil conversation with Ebony. "Yeah, I know your mother does hair, I remembered when we visit Chicago and I noticed all the great hair styles." Ebony said "Do you do your own hair, yours always looks good." Kara said. "Yeah I do my own, I've always liked to experiment on new styles." Ebony said. "Is that what you're going to do for a living Ebony?" "No, I can't." "Why, Ebony you can do what ever you want,

THE STEP FAMILY | 79

you don't have to do or be what anybody else says you have to be, and by the way about Roy, don't worry it's his loss." Kara said and got up in left the table. Then she heard Ebony say thank you in the background. Again here was this girl who wasn't a beauty queen, but was so confident and nice. That made Ebony wish that she was more like Kara. Kara had an inner beauty that showed all over her. The next few days the girls met every day at lunch. Ebony found herself laughing and being happy. "You know it's getting close before the end of the playoff and where down two games to three and there is a game tonight." Kara said. "I know how bad dad want to this win this season, I hope he wins tonight." "Why don't you come with us tonight Ebony, dad will be so happy to see you out there routing for him, unless you don't want to see Roy." "I now know I wasn't in love with Roy and it would have been bad for both of us if we had stayed together." "Right on, so what about it, will you come?" Kara asked. "Yes, I'll come!" Ebony said all excited.

That night Josh went over in picked Ebony up and he had Rita, Kara, Joey and Tommy all in the car smiling to see Ebony, as she got in the car. Tina watched from her upstairs window angry. "She got my husband now she want's my kids too, no this won't happen!" Tina said out loud. Ebony didn't know what to say but the family did. Joey jumped in her arms. "When you coming home?" he asked that broke her Ebony started crying from shame at how she treated these people and hurt from missing them. Rita was sitting next to her wiping her tears and held her while she unloaded. Then Tommy asked why Ebony was sad. "Those are happy tears." Kara explained. Ebony looked at Tommy and said "I'm sorry I hurt you, you're a good little boy, and you're my brother." Tommy and Joey both smiled with joy, everyone was happy. "Thank you Lord Things are now coming together." Rita said to her self.

When the family got to the arena in got their seats they were all excited and all the fans were talking about how they had to win this game. In the locker room the coach was trying to talk to the team in inspire them. "This is for all the marbles fellows we need to pull this off and just one more game after this, but we got to play like a team, all of us." Then he looked at Flex who just rolled his eyes. Joshua walked out to the floor with the team thinking. "Were going to lose this game unless a miracle happens, and then he saw it. Joshua looked up and saw his whole family even Ebony up in the stands smiling at him. Joshua with tears in his eyes couldn't help it, he walked right through the fans up to his family and one by one he hugged them all and when he got to Ebony she told him. "Dad you go whip their butts!" Joshua smiled as he hugged her and said "This one's for you baby." Joshua needed that extra push and he played his best game ever he scored forty points that game. The family was screaming out loud and Ebony had the best time. Then after the game Ebony didn't want to go to her mother's house so she stayed the night at the family's house and talked all night with Kara. Both of them finally, were getting that sister they always wanted. Joshua and Rita walked by Kara's room and heard them still talking. "Should we interrupt?" Joshua asked. "No, let them bond and besides, do you got any energy left big daddy?" Rita smiled coyly. "You know I always save some for you, what you got in mind." He grinned "Well I got to thank you for that great game you put on today, the way I do it." "And you know I like the way you say thank you, let's go baby." He said then they slipped into their bedroom, thinking today was a good day for the whole family.

The next morning was Saturday so Joshua decided to take the whole family out; first they went to a park where there were slides and rides. Joey and Tommy had so much fun they didn't want to leave. "I could just live here." Tommy said. "Me too!" Joey added. Later they went back to the house and Ebony got lesson on doing hair by Rita. Kara was the model; Ebony was so excited watching how Rita transformed Kara's hair. "Rita, would you teach me more, I would love to do hair." Ebony asked. "Than do it, I can get you into my shop and you can watch my people work and if your good enough I'll give you a job, oh I mean if you decide to come with us." Later Ebony laid in bed that night thinking how she didn't want to leave her mother but this was her chance to do something she wanted to do, instead of being just a pretty picture for some man to look at she could be her own person. And now she couldn't imagine being without her family. The next day the family all went to church and this time Ebony enjoyed the service, she could feel herself changing being around these people and it was good. That Sunday night Joshua dropped Ebony back at their mothers house and Tina was waiting for her.

CHAPTER TWELVE

WHOSE YOUR DADDY?

"SO GIRL YOU got you a new MAMA?' Tina said now drunk Ebony didn't answer and went straight for the stairs, she didn't want her mother to ruin her wonderful weekend. "Bring your ass back down these stairs!" Tina yelled. Ebony slowly walked down the stairs reluctantly. "What is it mother and please stop drinking!" Ebony yelled. "Don't you yell at me missy, and I can drink as much as I want, so I was wondering if you was gonna come back or was you going to stay with your step family." "Mother Rita and her kids are good people, I like them a lot and they like me and we all had the best weekend." "So I guess my ex husband was on top of the world, he got his new family and all of you and I got nothing." "Mother we love you, me and Josh and Joey and we will come back to see you as much as we can." "What are you talking about Ebony!" Tina yelled. "Well mother dad is leaving after the play off and moving back to Chicago and Josh and Joey are going and I think I'm gonna go too, Rita gonna teach me how to do hair." "What! How dare him think he can take all of you out of my life, he can't do it I'll take him to court!" "Mother let it go, you been so busy with Jack that months pass and you didn't even call." "So what I knew where you were and if I wanted to see you guys I didn't have to fly across the world to see you, he's just trying to hurt me. I won't let him get away with this!" Tina yelled.

The next morning Joshua was at home talking to Rita about their plans to move and how he was nervous about the next game. "Don't worry, you'll always have us, and I think Ebony wants to come with us now." Rita said. "Yes, baby that's what I wanted to hear, now I know were gonna win this last game then we will get out of here and go back home, I know your friends miss you." "Baby, Anna called me and told me she almost had to beat Glenda up, he wanted to bring all his ghetto fabulist stuff into the shop to decorate, but their doing well and had to hire another hair dresser to keep up with all of the clients." She said. "But everyone will be glad when your back. Thanks for making that sacrifice to stay here with me." Joshua smiled. "That's what families do." She smiled back. Then the phone rang. "What! No! What she can't!" Joshua yelled over the phone. Rita watched how her husband was yelling and very upset and wondered what could make him that angry. Joshua slammed down the phone and yelled. "That was my lawyer he got a call from Tina's lawyer, she heard about us leaving and now she gonna file a complaint so we cant take the kids out of the state and then she gonna file for custody for Ebony and Joey. Tina is just hating, she never cared about those kids before, now she want's to try to act like a mother!" Joshua yelled. "Calm down honey, let's try to figure out how we can work this out." Rita said trying to relieve the situation. "No, I'm calling that crazy woman right now!" Joshua yelled.

"Hello, who is this?" Tina asked. "You know who this is, you got caller ID, why are you doing this I got a call from my lawyer. Why do you want to stop the kids from coming with me you never cared before!" "Who do you think you are, you can't just take my children away from me to live with you and that tramp you married and her brats!" Tina yelled sending Joshua through the roof. "Tina don't you talk about my wife and our kids!" "Oh, so you claiming her kids, that's strange you never wanted to claim Joey!" Tina screamed and at this time Ebony heard her mother yelling and went to see what it was about, so Ebony stood outside the door in listen. "Yes I said it, you gonna claim her children but you never loved Joey, because he's Jack's child." Joshua was so upset said. "If that's the case why is he here, I've been taking care of you and your boy friends child all this time and you never said anything now you got a problem with it." "Yes, I do, now Josh Jr. is old enough to make his own decision, but Ebony and Joey you can't take them." "Tina let's, let Ebony make her own decision of who she want's to live with but as far as for Joey." Joshua took his time and said. "You can have him, he's your son." "No baby!" Rita yelled but it was too late, he had got it out of his mouth. "Come get him Tina!" Joshua said and hung up the phone. Ebony stood out side the door shaking "Joey is Jack's son, no that can't be true." She said to her self. Joshua looked at Rita who told him "We need to talk now" but neither one of them knew that soon as Joshua started yelling he was so loud everyone in the house could hear him, even two little boys standing outside the room. "What does daddy mean, he don't want me, and why can't I go with you Tommy?" Joey cried. "I won't let them take you away, you're my brother, and brothers help each other, come on let's go." Tommy said.

Joshua Jones we are going to have our first fight." Rita said. "Now baby, I know what your gonna say, but I can't keep Joey, if I tried that's Jack's son!" "No that's your

THE STEP FAMILY

83

son and you're the only father that boy knows you can't do that to him." "Rita you don't know how some times how bad it hurts to see this child that my ex wife had while she was with me. Laying in my bed and sleeping with another man, and when I held Joey in my arms after he was born, I was so happy to have another son. Until I found out how I was tricked, it hurt, but I took him in, and tried to forget the fact that Joey is some other man's son, but I cant forget." Joshua said sadly. "Well, let me ask you a question, you love The Rev, what if your biological father came knocking at this door and tried to claim you as his son, there would be a problem, wouldn't it." Rita said. Joshua thought about it and no way was there going to be anyone that could take the place of The Rev, but this was different from the beginning Tina knew this was Jack's child and she chose to keep it a secret from him.

Back at Tina's house Ebony was so hurt from hearing her mother's conversation. "Mother, how could you do this to dad, how can you do this to Joey!" Ebony shouted. "Do what, oh I guess you was ease dropping, I made a mistake and got pregnant by Jack, I could of aborted the baby but I didn't." she said. "Does Jack know that Joey is his son?" Ebony asked. "Yes he does." "And he doesn't even care and that's the kind of man, you want to be with, mother I'm ashamed of you and I am going with father and pray that I don't turn out like you!" Ebony cried in walked out the door. Tina felt like someone had stabbed her in the heart, her world was falling apart, and she knew she couldn't take Joey from the only family he knew and disrupt his life because she was hurting. A few moments later she heard the door close knowing her daughter just walked out of her life, Tina reached for her bottle to comfort her.

An hour later Ebony was at the family's home with her bags. When she saw her father she ran into his arms. "Dad I'm sorry for all the trouble I cause you when you was going through so much with my mother, I heard your phone call" she cried. Joshua held his daughter, he knew she had to find out one day, too bad it had to happen like it did, then Josh Jr. and Kara walked in and saw Ebony crying in her father's arms. "What's wrong now?" Josh asked. Josh stood still waiting to find out what the problem was. Joshua was thinking about how and what to say. "Tell him Joshua." Rita told him. "Tell me what?" Josh asked again. "It's Joey for years I thought about telling you and your sister that he's not my son he's Jack's" Joshua said sadly. "I know dad." "You knew?" Joshua asked surprised. "Dad I'm not naïve I saw Jack and I saw Joey and I know how long mom was involved with Jack and I put two and two together, but he's still my brother and he's still your son just like I am." Josh Jr. said "Wow, Josh I just saw you turn into a man right before my eyes, thanks son." Joshua said now feeling better after knowing that the secret about Joey was out. "Now no more talk about step families were just plain old family. Josh Jr., Ebony Kara, Tommy and Joey you're all brothers and sisters now is that clear!" Rita said forceful. "Yes maim." All the kids said, "Is that clear" Rita said again now looking at Joshua. "Yes maim." He said with his head down. Then the family all started laughing. "Now let's all sit down for dinner." Rita said "Okay I'll go get the boys" Kara said then went up stairs. A few moments later Kara came down stairs looking worried.

"The boys are not upstairs I looked every where, there probably hiding some where." After that the whole family searched the inside and outside the house and couldn't find them. Finally they figured out the boys had ran away. "They must have heard me on the phone with Tina and ran away because they didn't want to get separated." Joshua said worried, and then he called the police.

Miles away Tommy and Joey were getting off a bus walking toward the park they liked. "Joey you got any money?" Tommy asked. "No, I don't have any." Joey said. "Well I got three dollars and seventy eight cents." "That's a lot of money." Joey said. "I know we should be able to eat off this for a long time." Tommy said. "Are we ever gonna go back home Tommy?" Joey asked "Yeah when we get real big and they can't take us a part." Back at the house the police was there looking all around for signs, Joshua then had to call Tina.

"Tina, Joey and Tommy are missing I think they heard us arguing about Joey going to live with you and they ran away. I have the police here, but just in case they come there let us know quickly." Joshua said with sadness in his voice. "I'm so sorry Joshua this is all my fault." Tina cried. "No more arguing Tina, it just as much as mine, but we need to find my sons." Joshua said. That moment Tina felt like her eyes had open for the first time; here it was this man calling her child with another man his son. There was no way she could ever try to take any of her children from this wonderful man, they all loved him and she could see why. Tina got up in threw her bottle in the garbage and did something she saw Joshua do from time to time she got on her knees to pray. When Jack walked in Tina was sitting there with a new attitude and his bags packed at the door. "What's all this about?" he asked "This is about changing my life, our son Joey ran away, he's out there because he didn't want to come here with me and I had to look at myself and actually pray to understand that my whole life been a joke. Other than the children my life has been a nightmare. I thought all I had to do was be pretty and marry a rich man have his children and my life would be set. Then I met you and you brought excitement into my boring life and then I had Joey and not once did you step up in be a father or be a man, but that was my fault. I used Joshua then you used me and the bible says you reap what you sow. I'm reaping now because my oldest son doesn't come around my daughter is ashamed of me and now my little boy is out there running away from me. Now it's time for me to step up in be a mother to my children and the first thing I need to do is get rid of you." Tina said with complete confidence. "So what am I suppose to do?" Jack asked scared his luxury life style was coming to an end. "Go live off your other baby mama." Tina said and walked out the room. Jack grabbed his bags in walked out the door.

CHAPTER THIRTEEN

ON THE RUN

BACK AT THE house Ebony was in Kara's room; Kara had her in her arms while they both cried. Rita was in her room on her knees praying while Joshua and Josh Jr. were out driving around looking for the boys. After hours of driving around they had to come home. Josh Jr. went up to his room all tore down and defeated. Joshua sat by the phone, waiting for some word about his boys. Then it got late and Rita tried to get Joshua to go to sleep, but he told her he couldn't. Joshua sat up by the phone waiting for a call thinking how he wished both his sons were back at the house, no longer worrying about who the seed was for these two boys, those were his boys.

At the park it had got cold and dark. Tommy had bought him and Joey some potato chips and pop for dinner and as it got colder Tommy and Joey went into the outside bathroom to get out of the cold. The bathroom was dirty and nasty but it was warmer. As they sat there eating the boys heard some people coming so they ran into the back stall in closed the door. Tommy told Joey to not make a sound while a few men came in to do a drug buy. The boys listen how the men argued and cussed over the amount of money and the quantity of drugs. Then after finally agreeing, someone left the bathroom while a few stayed in and started smoking. The boys could smell the strong aroma of the drug then one of the fellows went into the next stall to use it. The boys was scared that the fellow would see them, but the fellows were so high and too busy thinking about the drugs, they didn't even bother to see if anyone else was in the bathroom. After the fellows left the boys sat down on the cold floor of the bathroom. It had got colder and Joey was shaking from the cold floor, Tommy then pulled his coat off and wrapped Joey up in it and held him and the two boys went to sleep.

The next morning Rita had cried and prayed all night and walked down stairs to see Joshua still sitting by the phone. "Joshua you got to get some sleep, you got a game tonight." She said. "Rita I can't play in the game with all this happening." "Baby there is nothing you can do now but pray and do your job, you got a lot of people depending on you tonight, we will find the boys." Joshua argued some more about it until he knew Rita was right, there was nothing he could do now but pray, and if he missed this last game it would be heart breaking not only to him, but to a lot of others.

That morning the boys couldn't wait to get out of that smelly bathroom, but by that afternoon Tommy had ran out of money and they were hungry. So Tommy started asking people that came into the park for money so they could buy some food. Most of the people just walked by the boys not caring about how these little boys were in the park without any adults around. Everyone just minding their own business, instead of calling the police, but there was this one man. The man was middle aged white and had lots of hair around his face, he was kind of chubby and he was wearing a long dark coat. He had been walking through the park and saw the boys and gave Tommy five dollars. "Thank you sir!" Tommy yelled thinking he was rich then he ran over to the store with Joey and bought more junk food. The two boys ate and played while that man that gave them the money sat on a bench back in the park in watched the kids. Later Joshua came down stairs looking so tired, Rita held her husband, "Look baby go do what you have to do, and we will stay here and wait for the boys to come home. Joshua kissed his wife and left out the door feeling so defeated, how he could have let this happen and wondering if his boys were okay.

A while later Rita heard a knock on the door, she ran to it thinking it might be the boys. When Rita open the door she was shocked to see Tina standing there. "Rita have you heard anything about the boys?" Tina asked. "Nothing yet, we are still looking and praying." Rita said. "Yes, I even had to get on my knees, I'm so worried Rita I don't know what I'd do if something happen to my son." "Me too, come in Tina, I know how you feel. It's so hard for a mother to have a son missing and try to hold it up for the rest of the family." "It sure is hard Rita, but everyone loves you, including my children and I know it's kind of late but I want to thank you for taking them in as your own. I don't know if I could of done that and I'm sorry for all the mean things I said or done to you and Joshua, you two belong together and I wish you much happiness please forgive me." Tina begged. "Tina I already have God said if you want to be forgiven you have to learn to forgive, I just pray we find our children and all of us will be happy including you Tina." "Thank you Rita" Tina said crying her eyes out worrying for her son and his brother and now how she misjudged this lady. "Rita can we pray." "Of course, but wait a minute we need some help." Rita then called all the kids downstairs. When Ebony saw her mother she ran into her arms. "I'm sorry for what I said to you mother I was so mad." Ebony cried. "I understand you was right and I gave Jack his walking papers." Tina said. "Finally!" Josh Jr. said relieved. Then went over and hugged his mother. "I called you kids down stairs because it's praying time. We need to pray for your father who is going to have the hardest night ever out there on the floor. And we have to pray for those boys where ever they are for God to keep a hedge around them." Rita said then they all held hands in Rita prayed. Everyone praying along with their hearts heavy. The tears were flowing in that house. Afterward they all sat down wondering where the boys could be. Then Josh Jr. yelled. "The park! Remember how the boys said how they liked that park, let's go!" So Josh Jr. Kara and Ebony got into his car to go look for their brothers.

Meanwhile back at the stadium the game had started and Joshua was tired and worried. After halftime the team was behind by twenty points. "What's wrong big man, you ain't got any juice, you want to go out a loser!" Flex yelled. Joshua just sat there too beat up to argue then walked out of the locker room. "What's wrong with him?" Flex asked. "His boys are missing, they ran away and JJ been up all night worrying about them." Roy said then added "Joshua is doing the best he can and if it wasn't for him we wouldn't have made it this far, he needs us to step up and play as a team for him and for his boys." Then the team left leaving Flex there thinking. "I got plenty of games to play, this is JJ last one." The third quarter started off different Houston was playing together. Flex was passing the ball to the open player and they were battling back, but most of the fans thought it was too late and that they were to far behind.

Back at the park it was getting dark again in the two boys were tired and cold, neither one of them wanting to sleep in that cold smelly bathroom again. "Where do we go now Tommy?" Joey asked "Let's see I got two dollars left, I know we can go to grand pa and grand Mama Kelly's house, they'll let us stay together. "Isn't it a long way, how we gonna get there?" Joey asked. "We go to the airport in get on an airplane." Tommy said. "Do we got enough money?" Joey asked. "No, I don't think so but there's that nice man that gave us five dollars maybe he'll help us." Tommy said.

The man name was Clarence Murray he was a divorced man with no children. Clarence worked at a meat factory and had just been let out of jail for child molestation. All Clarence life he grew up abuse being molested when he was young then in jail when he was a teenager. So when he was an adult having not been helped he would molest his young family members mostly the boys, until he got caught and left town and married a woman with a small boy. Clarence couldn't help his self he did it again touching that boy where he shouldn't have. His wife had him put in jail in divorced him. Clarence had only been out for a few months and watching these two boys in the park all day he was starting to get those sick urges. Clarence waited to see if some parent would come get the boys, he noticed how all these so called caring people walked away from these two boys and thought how they didn't care for these boys so he was going to take them home with him when it got dark. Clarence waited a little while later then walked toward the boys. "Sir Can you give us some money so me and my brother can go back home to Chicago?" Tommy asked. "Do your parents know where you're at little boy?" he asked. "No, me and my brother ran away were going to go and fly to Chicago, but we need some money, can you help us?" Tommy asked. "Sure I can come to my car in I'll drive you to my house and fix you some food then give you some money to go on the airplane." Tommy remembered what his mama said about not going with strangers but this man had gave them money and he had to make sure Joey had something to eat. "Okay, come on Joey" Tommy said and Joey grabbed his brother's hand while they walked with Clarence over to his car. Clarence smiled then opened the door, then he heard someone calling.

"Tommy, Joey, what are you doing!" Josh Jr. yelled having pulled up beside Clarence's car then jumped out his car followed by Kara and Ebony. The boys ran into their sister's arms now both cold tired and hungry. The girls were crying tears of joy. Josh looked at this man standing at his car wondering what he was going to do with his brothers. Clarence started lying. "Man, I was just going to bring the boy's home." He lied. Josh could see something strange about this man and how nervous he looked. "Where did they tell you where their home was?" Josh asked. "Oh, they didn't know the address they were going to point it out." Clarence lied again. "Joey might not know a lot of things, but both him and Tommy know where we live sir, what's your name?" Josh asked. Clarence knew he was caught so he started running, Josh took off after him and caught up with him and threw him to the ground. "You pervert what did you think you was going to do with my little brothers!" Then Josh Jr. started hitting Clarence in the face. Kara ran over and tried to stop Josh from killing the man while Ebony put the boys in the car and called the police. Minutes later the police got there and arrested Clarence in told the kids Clarence background. Kara and Ebony both in shock but relieved they got to the boys just in time.

Back home Rita and Tina was at the house sitting by the phone worrying about their sons when all the kids came busting through the door. Both mothers ran to their little boy and picked them up kissing and hugging them both crying tears of joy. "Mama don't whoop me, I just didn't want Joey to go away." Tommy cried. "Don't you worry Tommy, Joey will stay with you, along with his big brother and sisters, I

THE STEP FAMILY

89

wont separate you guys, but I expect you all to come up in visit me and call me every week." Tina cried. Ebony and Josh Jr. and Joey all hugged their mother, while Kara and Tommy were holding theirs. "Wait a minute we got to get to the game Dads needs our help!" Josh Jr. said hearing about the game on the radio. "Well I guess I'll go home" Tina said. "No you come with us, Joshua needs all the help he can get." Rita said. So they all piled in Josh Jr. big range rover in sped down to the stadium.

On the floor the team had rallied back, they were only two points behind. The team fought hard while Joshua sat on the bench tired and overwhelmed of the loss of his sons then after Flex fouled out Joshua had to go in. Flex had played so hard to catch the team back up. Joshua saw that. "Come on big man go out a champion." Flex said to Joshua as he grabbed his towel, then shook Joshua's hand. Joshua was still numb, but got in the game. Joshua legs was like jelly, but he made it down to the basket in Roy passed the ball in with all his strength Joshua jumped up in stuffed the ball, on the way up, one of the other players grabbed at his arm and fouled him. It was now ninety-nine to ninety nine on the score board. No more time left on the clock, Joshua was so tired he could hardly keep his eyes open, his arms felt like they had weights on them holding them down. Joshua could hear his team yelling, "One shot, One shot!" Then the fans started yelling "One shot!" Then it got quiet while Joshua bounced the ball on the floor then went up to take his last shot then he heard. "Dad you whip their butts!" Joshua turned his head in saw Rita, Josh Jr., Kara Ebony, the boys! And even Tina there all smiling. Right then Joshua second wind hit in and he smiled in said. "This is for you family!" Then threw the ball up, the ball hit the rim then rolled around then finally fell in. The crowd went berserk. Everyone was running out on to the floor. Joshua made his way to his family. Everyone was cheering and jumping up in down. Joshua first grabbed his two little boys both in his arms and hugged them as tears fell down his face. The fans thinking it was because they had won the champion ship, but these tears were for his little boys. Joshua was so overwhelmed with all his family there. Tina walked over to him and Rita and gave him a friendly hug while the kids watched. "Joshua you go back home to Chicago and watch over my children all of them and I'm hoping the best for all of you." Tina said. "Thank you Tina and we'll be praying for the best for you also." Joshua said holding on to his wife and children. Tina walked away smiling and thinking this was the first day of her new life.

After all the hoopla the family all went home. Josh Jr. was in his room sleeping while the girls were in Kara's room still talking about boys, clothes and girl things. While the two boys after eating a big dinner was sound asleep in their room. Joshua and Rita lay across their bed in each other's arms. "What a day, I'm glad it's over and now my beautiful wife I can't wait to go back home with all our family, and you know where going to need a big huge house. Josh Jr. will be living with us while he goes to college and the girls will finish high school, but the boys Tommy and

Joey will keep us busy for a long time." Joshua smiled "Not as long as this one is." Rita said then put Joshua's hand on her stomach. "You mean another one!" Joshua yelled. "Yes another one" Rita smiled. Then Joshua jumped out the bed yelling "were gonna have a baby!" Then all the kids came running in the room. Everyone excited to be having a new addition to the family. Then Joey asked. "Daddy can our new baby not be a step baby?" Everyone was getting misty as Joey brought home some wisdom. Joshua looked at his family all together and happy and said. "As of now In the Jones home there is no longer and will never be step family in our home, we are just plain old family."

The End by Janette A Rucker
September 30, 2008

ABOUT THE AUTHOR

MY NAME IS Janette A Rucker and I just hit the big 50 and I've been [...] to have grown up with two wonderful parents my father Robert Andrews Sr. [...] gone to glory but was the best father a child/adult could ask for. My mother [...] Andrews is a beautiful exciting spicy woman (I won't tell her age) but she [...] ood!" That's my mama!" My husband Robert Lee Rucker is my prince and [...] that I have been married to for over twenty five years. And my life for the [...] has been good, but at the darkest time of my life I started writing and it [...] rough and after the first two novels I couldn't stop. My prayer is I touch [...] heart and tell them how good God is and every situation but I do at times [...] because I want to keep it real and make you laugh at the same time. So [...] ou will enjoy this book and the others to come.

Thanks peace and love

Janette A Rucker.